Lois,

Hope you enjoy
My Book!

UNSOLVED CASE

SYD SULLIVAN

ARCHWAY
PUBLISHING

Archway Publishing books may be ordered through booksellers or by contacting:

Archway Publishing
1663 Liberty Drive
Bloomington, IN 47403
www.archwaypublishing.com
1 (888) 242-5904

Front Cover Image: Tyler Lord, Illustrator

ISBN: 978-1-4808-7116-8 (sc)
ISBN: 978-1-4808-7115-1 (e)

Library of Congress Control Number: 2018963154

Print information available on the last page.

Archway Publishing rev. date: 11/12/2018

Honorable Mentions

Thank you to my parents, my sister Danielle, and my mentor, Chris. This wouldn't have been possible without your love and support.

1

CRIME SCENE

It was a cool fall evening in Dorchester, Massachusetts, and police were investigating a crime scene where a young couple had just been murdered. They had received a 911 call at 2243 hours about an intruder in the home. By the time police arrived at the scene, it was too late.

A police officer broke through the front door with gun in hand and found the young couple lying dead on the floor. It was clear that they had been murdered because they showed no movement, and puddles of blood as red as roses stained the carpet.

Detective Smith searched through the house for more evidence. Smith had just started working as a detective, but before that he had been a regular police officer who had wanted to protect his town.

Smith had no luck finding any evidence in the first floor of the home, and so he decided to look for evidence upstairs. He walked past the two dead bodies in the living room while stepping over a pool of blood from one of the victims. The remaining officers concealed the victims by using black body bags. The victims were later going to be examined by the autopsy department to find the cause of death.

Smith knew by looking at the wounds that the two victims had been stabbed to death. Almost getting choked up at seeing his two best friends lying on the floor dead, Smith knew he had to find another person who lived in this house: the child who belonged to this couple. Not knowing the whereabouts of the child concerned him tremendously.

Smith thought, *Normally when I walk into a crime scene where someone has died, I don't feel an intense pain in my chest like I do now. The job today is remarkably different. When it's someone you know, someone you care about, it really hits home.*

While walking to the stairs, Smith noticed that the front door of the house was open. It was a double door, and both sides were open. He saw a neighbor down the street giving another police officer a report. The witness was an older man with gray hair and square glasses.

Smith saw that more people who lived down the block were concerned and wanted to see what had happened. Police officers had to keep them back from the area, and so they all gathered behind the yellow police tape that surrounded the crime scene.

Smith squinted at all of the flashing blue and red lights, remembering why he had gotten started in the police force in the first place. He'd needed a good job to help provide a good life for his wife and two sons. For years he had always wanted to be a father, and then his wife gave birth to twins. Right after he got the detective position, his two boys were born. He was glad to also have a job for which his family would be proud of him.

Having that in mind, Smith turned from the door to go up to the second floor of the residence. Step by step, his shiny black shoes walked up the stairs. Since he had received the detective position, he had traded in his police uniform for a suit and tie.

When he got to the top, there were three different rooms to investigate. First, he pushed open the door that was directly in front of him. As he opened the door, he saw a beach-themed bathroom with seashells and seahorses painted on the walls. The walls were light blue, and the shower curtain had all types of fish and underwater creatures. He looked throughout the whole bathroom, discovered no evidence, and closed the door behind him.

He ventured down the hallway and into the room on his left. He opened the door to a bedroom with a bed dressed in a maroon quilt and soft white pillows. He assumed that this was the victims' room. As they were collecting the victims, he couldn't help but notice the ring on the young women's finger as she was put into a body bag. They were a newlywed couple. He was hoping that he was going to find some evidence here.

When he got to the center of the room, he heard a cry coming from within. He second-guessed what he was hearing but wondered where it came from. Suddenly, he heard the noise again. His head turned toward the sound. It was coming from the closet. He identified the sound as a small infant's cry. Having two newborn babies at home, he knew the sound well.

He put his hand on the side of the closet and cracked it open slowly. He breathed with a sigh of relief that what he saw wasn't scary or horrifying.

His eyes gazed upon a baby girl who appeared to be about three months old. He guessed she was crying from being in a dark closet for who knew how long. She wore a pink shirt with a diaper and no shoes and was lying down on a blanket.

Her skin was porcelain white, and she was just starting to grow some blonde hair. As she cried, tears rolled down her cheeks. Smith instantly lifted her up from her blanket and pulled her close, trying to comfort her.

He patted her on the back, trying to get her to stop crying. A bunch of scenarios went through his mind all at once. How had she survived and not her parents? How long had she been up here? He was glad that she was not like other victims he had seen downstairs.

He then yelled, "Neil, get up here!" He heard Neil's footsteps running up the stairs. Neil peeked around the corner in concern.

He gazed with surprise upon the child in Smith's arms and said, "Where didja find 'er?"

With the baby still crying, Smith answered, "I found her cryin' in the closet. Her parents are gone, Neil."

Neil said in shock, "We need to give 'er to social services."

"No, that won't be necessary, Neil. I am her godfather."

Neil said, "Okay. I'll make a report that the infant was found." Neil then ran back down the stairs to alert his fellow officers on what his orders were.

Smith stood up with the baby in his arms, saying, "You're okay. You're gonna be okay." He kneeled back down, grabbed the blanket from the floor, and wrapped her in it to keep warm. Smith had found a very important witness in this case, but sadly she couldn't tell them what she might have seen.

As Smith wrapped her up, he noticed some writing on the side of the blanket. Written in cursive pink letters was, "Ariel." He was relieved that he had found her, and he wasn't going to let anything happen to her. Ariel was his goddaughter, and her parents were dead, so he was the next person to take care of her.

Smith was sad to know that her parents weren't going to be able to see her grow up. He then thought that she shouldn't have to go to foster care and grow up not knowing what had really happened to her parents.

Smith put the crime scene together as he held Ariel in his arms. Her mother must have put her in that closet when the intruder had entered the house. She'd hidden her because it was a mother's mission to always protect her children no matter what.

The house where the crime had taken place was the very first house on Elm Street. When one turned onto Elm Street, it was the first house on the right, and the strip went along for about a mile and a half farther down the street. Land was up for sale all the way down this strip. Now that a murder had taken place in that residence, potential buyers would probably never want to live next door.

2

DREAM ON

Sadly, the murderer was never found. Smith and the other detectives tried to crack the case, but it couldn't be done. Whoever did this was smart, and he or she knew what he or she was doing. No fingerprints, DNA, or possible murder weapons were found. The very evil and clever person had covered the tracks.

That was all fifteen years ago. Smith, the detective who had found the baby girl, grew very fond of her. He took in his goddaughter as one of his own, legally adopting her. At the time that Ariel's parents had died, his boys had just been born, but he had always envisioned having a daughter. His boys were only three months younger than Ariel when he'd found her in September.

He knew that growing up in foster care was no life for a child, and he didn't want to see another child go through that. When Smith adopted her, she became one of the family.

Mr. and Mrs. Smith had talked about having more kids, but they thought that they were going to have their hands full enough with two boys.

Once Mrs. Smith heard about Ariel's story, she couldn't say no to her husband. The glimmer that she saw in his eyes when he told her about adopting Ariel was remarkable.

The whole Smith family decided that they were going to treat Ariel as if she were one of their own. At first it took some time getting used to. Three toddlers under one roof was a tremendous challenge at times. Several times through the night, they would hear whining babies. Some nights Mr. or Mrs. Smith wouldn't get more than an hour of sleep. Just as one baby would finally fall asleep, another would wake up. Mr. Smith would have to go to work the next day, and no amount of coffee could perk him up.

Some days, raising three kids the same age could be trying. That was three lunches a day he have to make for them to go to school. Three kids to drive to sports and after-school activities. Three different personalities when it came to what movie or TV show to watch on a Friday night. Three kids to drive him insane sometimes. But there were also many joys with children.

It was Sunday morning in the Smith residence. Mr. Smith had just gotten out of bed and was making himself some coffee. After a few minutes, his coffee was ready, and he took a sip. The first sip of a cup coffee was the best. No other beverage tasted better than coffee in the morning.

After that first sip, he turned and walked down the hall. He realized Ariel's door was cracked open. He walked by Aaron and Eric's room. He couldn't tell them apart just by looking at them. The only difference was Eric had a four-inch scar on his ribs when he'd broken them skate boarding. But before Eric got that scar, they had to dress in different clothes every day. If they did wear the same clothes, it would be impossible to tell them apart.

Aaron and Eric both had the same green eyes. They stared into one's soul and shimmered in the darkness. They had the same color hair and hairstyle. However, Aaron was more of a flirt with the ladies, whereas Eric was more intelligent and shy.

As Mr. Smith went down the hallway to close Ariel's door,

he peeked inside to see her sleeping. She was curled up in a ball, facing the wall with her quilt wrapped around her. He shut the door and continued walking down the hallway with a smile on his face, thinking of how far she had come since the day he'd adopted her.

Inside Ariel's head, however, she was having a terrible nightmare. Usually, when she had a nightmare, she kicked and screamed, and her parents usually woke her up. This time, it was different.

You know when you have a dream where you feel like it's so real, you think its reality, or it's so terrible you want to wake up from it? We never know why we have happy dreams or sad dreams. Even when we have nightmares, we can't help but think why we dream about certain events.

Ariel's nightmare was about how her family had turned against her and put her out on the streets. When she woke up, she let out a gasp so loud that her dad heard her when he was in the hallway. He ran in saying, "You okay?"

Ariel said, "Yeah, it was just a dream. I'm sorry."

"Not another one," he said. Ariel nodded. Smith felt bad for what went on inside her head at night. He sat next to her on the bed and wrapped his arms around her. "It's just a dream."

Ariel realized what she had just woken up from and said, "Dad you and Ma would never kick me out of the house, right?"

Her dad looked down at her in surprise. "Ariel, sweetie, I would never do that. As long as you don't steal your mom's nail polish, you'll be fine. Ariel, I need you, and not just to keep your brothers in line."

Ariel smiled about how sometimes she was the normal child in the family compared to her brothers. Aaron and Eric were sometimes clowns, but she loved them to death anyway. Smith hugged her once more, and they were happy to be in each other's lives.

Then an abundance of laughter and noise came from the hallway. They both thought to themselves that Aaron and Eric were awake.

Ariel and her dad realized that Aaron and Eric were watching them hugging on the bed. They thought to say something stupid to stop this touching moment. The twins tended to do that a lot.

Eric said, "Oh, dear, Ariel. Did the monster try to kill you in your dreams again?" He then stuck out his bottom lip to imply that she was still a baby for having nightmares. Even though Ariel was fifteen, she still had bad dreams. Everyone got them, and she knew that it was completely normal, but she had them at every other night. *Is that normal for people?* she thought.

Aaron laughed beside him and said, "Naw, she's just upset about how she hasn't grown since she was a baby." Eric burst out laughing about Ariel's shortness.

Ariel didn't find it funny at all. She was being terrorized by two freakishly tall demons. Aaron and Eric were both six foot five. For fifteen, that was giant height. Her dad was six foot four, but the only person she could relate to was her mom. Ariel's mom was five foot seven. Even though her mom was seven inches taller than her, they stood together to hear all the short jokes.

Finally her dad said, "All right, that's enough, you two! Come on. Let's have some breakfast." Aaron and Eric bolted for the kitchen. Those two were always hungry considering their height and weight.

Ariel got out of bed and put on her robe and slippers. Then she really thought about how it was weird that she didn't get her father's height. Sometimes Ariel had to buy clothes in the kids section because they don't have clothes in her size. That was how petite she really was—or as Eric would say, elf size.

She proceeded to the hallway, hoping that Aaron and Eric hadn't eaten everything already. *Just because they're tall doesn't give them the right to eat the entire fridge,* Ariel thought.

Ariel sat on a bar stool and yawned quietly. The kitchen had marble countertops with black cabinet doors and silver handles on the doors. A black stove and white marble sink were in between the cabinets.

Above that sink was a window overlooking the city. There were cars moving in every direction even though it was an early Sunday morning. They lived in an apartment building in Boston. Their apartment was on the top floor, and they could see the whole city from that kitchen window. They could see hundreds of cars driving in and out of Boston. They almost looked like ants from the window because the apartment building was so high off the ground.

They could see the Tobin Bridge and the TD Garden, home of the Celtics and the Bruins. Also, they could see the beautiful Zakim Bridge, which was quite a view when the whole bridge was lit up at night. If they looked more west, they could see the Prudential, which was one of the tallest buildings in Boston. From time to time, they saw and heard planes flying in and out of Logan Airport.

Mr. Smith enjoyed serving his wife breakfast in bed on Sunday mornings. She worked so hard during the week, and he rewarded her for doing so much for him. She was a very loving mother to the kids. That was mainly from being the oldest of seven children, and so she has the motherly instinct within her. Even when she went to work, she was a mother to all her students. She was a teacher at her kids' school, and she taught geography, which was Aaron's favorite subject. The best thing about having her for a teacher was that she didn't give out much homework.

Eric was basically a young Albert Einstein. He was the smartest kid in school, but he didn't like to flaunt his intelligence. Around his teachers, his true self could surface. He was the kind of person that liked to be quiet and have his work speak for him.

Aaron was given the label of jock at his school because if one named a sport, he played it. Also, finding time to go out with cheerleaders on Friday nights was a struggle. His favorite sport was basketball. He spent hours of his day watching basketball videos on YouTube. He was inspired by watching and learning from great NBA players. He hoped that one day he'd be in the NBA. That was his number one goal in life.

Ariel was completely different than her brothers. She wasn't really good in sports, but she enjoyed them. She wasn't very coordinated, but she played basketball when she was younger. Because Aaron and Eric played basketball, she'd wanted to try it out.

She liked it for a while, but when she got into middle school, she started disliking being on the team. A lot of the other girls grew taller than her, and everyone who was on the team bullied her. She tried to go to the coach about how everyone on the team was treating her, but that didn't help.

The coach thought Ariel was making up lies about everyone on the team to get sympathy. Ariel couldn't stand their harsh words anymore, and so she didn't try out in the winter. The coach never asked her why she didn't try out. He was probably glad that she didn't come.

Ariel was the shortest girl on the team, which made her be teased more and feel uncomfortable. They made fun of her so often because she was no use to the basketball team. Now, she was still five feet tall and still hoping she'd grow at least a few more inches before she went to college.

Ariel didn't know what she wanted to do with her life just yet. There was a lot to choose from. Luckily she still had plenty of time to figure that out.

Back in the kitchen, Ariel looked beside her and saw that her brothers already had huge plates of food for breakfast. They had scrambled eggs, bacon, Pop Tarts, pancakes, and tall glasses of orange juice.

Ariel looked at them and said, "You guys know if you keep eating all that junk, you're going to get fat."

Aaron and Eric looked at each and laughed while they shoved more bacon into their mouths. Aaron said, "We need a lot of food to fill our tall bodies. Unlike someone else I know." They laughed again with their mouths full and high-fived each other.

Their dad turned around laughing a little, but he tried to hide it so Ariel wouldn't see him laughing about their joke. He looked at

Ariel's face and could tell that she was mad. He said, "All right, boys, that's enough short jokes for the day." Then he and the boys burst out laughing at Ariel's face, which looked as if flames were about to start coming out of her ears.

She was so over all the jokes about her. She had thought of coming up with some tall jokes, but they weren't any good. *Come on. Being short is awesome, and for people who aren't, it's just sad.* She wasn't exactly the best at coming up with jokes, and so she had to find a way to accept it.

Luckily, Allison came around the corner and said, "Come on, guys. Stop picking on Ariel like that. Mornin', hun." She hugged Ariel from behind. Then she made her way down the bar stools, patting her boys on their shoulders. "Mornin', boys."

They both said, "Morning," with mouths full of pancakes and syrup.

Ariel was mortified that she was related to these two idiots. They had no class at all and always ate like pigs.

Allison then made her way over to her handsome husband and gave him a kiss on the cheek. He said, "Mornin', honey. I made a fresh pot of coffee."

Once she poured herself a cup, she made her way past Ariel and realized she wasn't eating anything yet. "Ariel, honey, why aren't you eating anything?"

Ariel said, "Because these clowns ate everything already!"

Aaron replied, "You snooze, you lose." Then he went back to eating his pancakes.

Her dad said, "Ariel, I'll make you some oatmeal." Ariel was relieved that finally she was going to have some breakfast.

Eric came up for some air from eating and said, "Oatmeal? Come on, sis. You mean that slop you eat? Why don't you eat something that has flavor to it for once?"

Ariel said, "Because unlike you two, I actually care what I put in my body." They both stopped eating wildly, and Ariel finally got her oatmeal. After a couple spoonfuls, Ariel asked her parents, "Oh, can I go over to Chelsea's apartment today and hang out?"

Her parents said it was okay, but right before she could say anything else, her brothers interrupted like they always did. Aaron said, "Is Chelsea that hot cheerleader? What time are you going over there? Does she like me?"

Eric said, "No, Aaron, she likes me."

Ariel finished her oatmeal and ignored her brothers' stupid and inappropriate questions. Then she headed back to her room before anything else happened. She slammed her bedroom door and locked it before her brothers could enter her room. Aaron started saying, "Come on, Ariel! Can you just see if she likes me or not? That would be awesome. The 'best sister of the year' award will have your name on it!"

Eric said, "No, see if she likes me, Ariel. Please?"

Ariel kept ignoring them and went into her bathroom, leaving them yelling in the hallway. She let them think she was listening, but she really wasn't.

Yawning, she thought, *For one day, could they both just be normal human beings? Yet, who is really normal, anyway? We're all different in some sort of way, whether it's the way we talk, the way we look, or how we act. There is one thing that everyone in the world has in common: we all are human, and we all have imperfections.*

3

SPY GUYS

Ariel was excited to go over to Chelsea's place. Chelsea was her best friend from school. Ariel didn't have many friends from her school, but Chelsea was someone she'd always have a friendship with.

Ariel remembered one day when Chelsea saw her crying on the playground after school. Chelsea knew something was wrong, and so she walked over to her. "Ariel, are you okay?"

Ariel wiped her tears off her cheek and looked up at Chelsea. Chelsea saw that Ariel had a swollen eye and a cut lip. She gasped in shock. "Oh, my god, Ariel! Who did this to you?"

At first Ariel wouldn't say. She was so embarrassed about what had happened. It was the basketball team who'd hurt Ariel. They'd hurt her because they wanted her to quit the team. Eventually, Chelsea found out who did that to Ariel and went to the principal. The principal expelled the girls who were responsible. That didn't stop them from bothering her, though. Ariel and Chelsea became best friends that day. Before they had been acquaintances who knew each other from class.

When Ariel was in the shower, she thought about all the times Chelsea had stuck up for her. Chelsea had a short brown hair cut to her shoulders, and she had hazel eyes. She was only a little taller than Ariel, and so they both took on the short jokes everyone said to them.

Even though Chelsea and Ariel were close friends, Ariel had always been secretly jealous of her. Chelsea would date all the hot guys and get special treatment from them. She would receive roses in the hallway from the guy she was currently dating. Ariel then questioned how they were really close. When one thought about it, they were total opposites. *Is it possible opposites attract? I guess so.* The day Chelsea had found Ariel on the playground, they'd decided to always watch out for each other.

Ariel again wondered why she didn't look like her parents or have her dad's height. She felt that her parents were keeping a secret from her. She was scared but curious about the situation. Every time she brought up the subject, her parents would always dance around the issue and act peculiar.

Ariel stepped out of the shower and wrapped a warm towel around her. Then she grabbed a small comb and worked on her hair. She spent over a hundred dollars a month for hair care products to keep her dirty blonde hair luscious and healthy. She loved her long blonde hair because it gave her a feeling that she was like Rapunzel from the Disney movie *Tangled*. Rapunzel was Ariel's favorite Disney princess.

After Ariel got completely ready, she had a feeling Aaron and Eric were still outside her door waiting for her. She guessed that they wanted to ask her more stupid questions about Chelsea. Before she left, she looked in the mirror one last time. She had light blue jeans on with her black army boots. Ariel's shoe size was also hard to find, especially when she wanted to find adult shoes. She was only a five and a half, or size six for boots. She wore a black and green Boston Celtics T-shirt to match her boots.

Ariel straightened her long blonde hair. When she straightened her hair, it reached all the way down to her lower back. She ran her fingers through her hair and felt confident.

"Excuse me, boys," Ariel said upon opening her door. She looked up at them as if they didn't intimidate her. She slipped in between her two brothers to get in the hallway.

"Hey, come on, Ariel. I'll hook you up with Celtics tickets. I know a guy who can get courtside seats!" Aaron felt empowered, trying to get Ariel to take the bait.

She turned around and said, "Aaron, I can get tickets myself. I also know a guy, but unlike my guy, he isn't imaginary. I'm not going to hook you up with Chelsea!" Then she grabbed her phone and stuck it in the back pocket of her jeans. She took her wallet off the kitchen counter and walked toward the door.

Eric said, "So will you give Chelsea my number?" Eric felt confident about asking nicely this time, hoping that Ariel would say yes.

Ariel answered, "Yeah, fat chance. Tell Ma and Dad I'll be back in a few hours." She slammed the door behind her.

Aaron and Eric were the devil twins from hell according to Ariel, but she wasn't the only one who called them that. They would often prank their teachers in school. One time, Aaron broke into the school and wrapped everything in his math class with wrapping paper. That included the desks, the chairs, and everything that was on his teacher's desk. Another teacher got pranked for giving Aaron a bad grade on a test. When she opened her car door, paint came spilling out like Niagara Falls. Aaron basically said that she gave them too much homework on the behalf of the entire class. Instead of getting in trouble, they were rewarded with more homework than usual.

Another time in chemistry class, Aaron put a flammable substance in his teacher's coffee when he wasn't looking. Right as the teacher was about to take a sip, it blew up in his face. He was fine now and only got first-degree burns, as Aaron pointed out. He was trying to get him and the rest of the class out of taking a horrible test. No one was ready for it, of course, and so Aaron thought about the fame he would get for getting everyone not to take the test. Aaron did not confess to what he did, and the principal decided to suspend everyone who was in that class. Instead of getting fame, he was shunned by everyone in class for two weeks. Even his own brother thought he took things a little too far. It took place on April Fool's Day, and so Aaron didn't think it was that big of a deal. God help their teachers when it was senior prank week at their school.

Aaron and Eric looked at each other as if they had the same idea running through their minds. Eric said, "I'm so glad you're my brother."

Aaron said, "I know," with an evil smile.

They both said at the same time, "Fire escape."

Chelsea's apartment was only two floors down. Ariel took the elevator to get to Chelsea's place. Her apartment number was 802.

When she was in the elevator, she realized that they'd redecorated the interior. It was a modern look with white tiled floor and mirrorlike walls. The elevator stopped on the eighth floor, the doors opened, and she walked out.

She turned to the left, walking down a long hallway and passing several other doors along the way. When she got to Chelsea's door, she knocked quietly. Within a few moments, Chelsea answered the door and said, "Hey, come on in!"

They hugged in the doorway, and Ariel said, "Hey, how are ya?"

"Great! My parents are out of town on business, so I have the whole apartment to myself this weekend."

Ariel thought, *Wow, that must be nice to have the whole place to yourself sometimes. Aaron and Eric are always around, it seems—and if they're not there, my parents are always home.*

Even if she was an only child, her parents wouldn't leave her alone. Ariel wondered why her parents were so protective of her. *I mean, yeah, they love me, but they let Aaron and Eric do whatever they want. They can go out after the sun goes down. Even though they've gotten into trouble in the past, I don't know why Mom and Dad even trust them. Aaron especially—he's such a loose cannon.*

One time they left Aaron and Eric home alone for only an hour, and the whole house was wrecked when they got back. That was a while ago, when Ariel was only twelve. When they had entered the apartment, Ariel was holding her third place trophy, and it was like a whole zoo had gone through the place. There was paper flying through the air, and music blasted so loudly that they couldn't hear themselves think. Even some furniture was tipped over. There were also feathers floating in the air, probably from a massive pillow fight. Aaron and Eric hadn't come along because they'd promised their parents that they were old enough to stay home by themselves. Obviously, Mr. and Mrs. Smith were wrong to trust them.

Ten cans of soda were empty on the kitchen floor. That was what made them run around, all crazy and energized. Since that day, they were never allowed to be left home by themselves, and they also had to attend all of Ariel's recitals and extra activities. They didn't like it, but their mom wasn't going to come home to a mess every time she left to do something with Ariel. She couldn't believe that her sons ran around like wild animals. They hadn't had one sip of soda since then. If they did, their mom would have their heads, like the Red Queen from *Alice in Wonderland*.

Ariel and Chelsea sat on her couch and watched some Netflix. Right behind them was a slider door leading to the patio. Outside the door were Aaron and Eric, climbing down the fire escape. This was just the first step in their evil plan.

Every time Ariel said she was going to Chelsea's, they spied on her from the fire escape. Today, they wanted to see what the girls were doing. Luckily, they weren't good at reading lips. Eric said to Aaron, "What are they saying?"

Aaron quickly spun around and said, "Will you be quiet? I'm trying to listen!" Then he turned back to Ariel and Chelsea.

Aaron and Eric had a huge crush on Chelsea. They found her very attractive and smart, like every other boy did at school. If they both started dating her, they knew that eventually she would have to choose between them.

Even though Aaron and Eric were brothers, they had a very healthy relationship with each other. They would compete in everything they do. They'd officially made winning Chelsea a competition years ago. They were worried that this competition might break up there closeness as brothers, and they didn't want to mess up anything.

Aaron decided that he wanted to get a better look, and so he climbed farther down the fire escape. The farther he went down the fire escape, the more exposed he was to Ariel and Chelsea if they turned around.

Aaron watched Ariel get more comfortable on the couch, and suddenly she turned her head, spotting Aaron on the fire escape.

She was so tired of their stubbornness. Her mouth dropped with anger, and her eyes widened. She then said, "Chelsea, I'll be right back. I need to get some air."

Chelsea said, "Okay," and paused the episode they were watching.

When Ariel got closer to the sliding door, Aaron's smile grew bigger, hoping she wouldn't get too upset with him. Eric hid behind Aaron's back, hoping Ariel only saw Aaron. He hated getting in trouble for Aaron's actions, but he'd gotten used to it over the years.

She shut the door quietly and said, "You guys can't be serious! What are you doing here?"

Eric then realized that his hiding place wasn't good, and so he came out of hiding and sat on the step above his brother.

Aaron quickly thought up a lie. "Bird-watching."

Ariel raised her eyebrows as if she knew that's wasn't what they were doing. "Really? Bird-watching? On Chelsea's part of the fire escape?"

Chelsea was behind her and said, "Well, bird-watching sounds extremely sarcastic."

Aaron said, "No, really!" Then he held up his binoculars. Obviously, they were being used to get a closer look inside the apartment, but Aaron couldn't tell truth.

Ariel turned around to Chelsea with an apologetic look.

There was an awkward moment of silence, and then Eric said, "Well, that was enough of bird-watching for one day." They both sprinted up the fire escape. "Bye, sis. Bye, Chelsea." They reached the top the building and crawled back through the window to their living room.

Ariel saw Aaron shut the window. "Man I am going to kill them when I get home!"

4

UNTOLD TRUTH

Chelsea said, "They were spying on us, weren't they?"

Ariel was confused by her naïveté. "Yes! This isn't the first time this has happened, Chelsea. I just couldn't take it any longer." They went back inside.

Chelsea said, "Why do your brothers spy on us when we hangout? I bet they're just trying to be protective brothers, right?" Chelsea felt smart, feeling that she understood why Ariel's brothers were protective of her.

Ariel said, "Protective of me? That's the last thing that they would do! The only reason they've been doing this is because they both have crushes on you!"

There was a silent pause in the room before Chelsea said, "Your brothers have a crush on me?"

Ariel was mad at her for acting surprised. Almost every guy at school had a crush on her. She thought, *How you could you be so blind when guys are trying to do everything in their power to win your affection?* "Yes, Chelsea, they do." She put her arms up in the air as if she was mad at something. "Chelsea, every boy who goes to our school has a major crush on you. Well, except the gay guys. But *almost* every boy at our school is deeply in love with you. Chelsea, you're every boy's dream. I can't believe you don't recognize it!"

Ariel wished she could taken back what she'd just said or turn back time, but she couldn't. She continued. "Chelsea, you're very beautiful, and I'm jealous of you. You get so much attention from everybody, not just boys. The teachers too."

Before Ariel could finish, Chelsea said, "Oh, you would just love to have my life, wouldn't you?" Her eyes filled up with tears. "My parents are out almost every night, gone almost every weekend, because their jobs keep them so damned busy! I don't get that much attention, Ariel. You should be lucky you have a family that loves you and cares about you. You're my only true friend who cares about me. You think it would be great to have my life, but it's not that fun for me!"

They both took back what they said, hugged, and cried it out. They started laughing again by looking up some cat videos on YouTube. It turned out Chelsea was mad that her parents didn't spend much time with her. Ariel comforted her and realized what an amazing family she had two floors up.

They both shared a gallon of chocolate ice cream with caramel and hot chocolate on top. They laughed while going down memory lane and seeing how they had become great friends. Beside Aaron and Eric, it turned out to be a pretty decent day.

When it was time for Ariel to go home for dinner, they were sad because they realized tomorrow was Monday, which was the worst day of the week.

When Ariel got home, her mom was cooking dinner in the kitchen. Ariel said, "Hey, Mom, where's Dad?"

Her mom took a break from making dinner and said, "He's in the bathroom, I think. Hey, Ariel, can Dad and I talk to you for a minute?"

Ariel said, "Sure." She hadn't done anything wrong recently. *Maybe they just want to talk?*

Ariel took off her shoes and sat on the couch. Her brothers were playing video games on the big, flat-screen TV. Eric felt bad about what had happened today. He felt extremely guilty because he had lost Ariel's trust. He said, "Ariel, I'm really sorry about today. If it makes you feel better, I know who has a crush on you."

Ariel was still boiling about what happened earlier. "Yeah, like anyone would have a crush on me!"

Eric looked at Aaron and said, "I tried, man."

Aaron's turned red as he said, "Shut up!" He smacked Eric on the shoulder.

Ariel didn't know what they were talking about. "Can you guys go away, please? Mom and Dad need to talk to me about something."

They thought about saying something stupid or inappropriate, but instead they simply turned off the TV and went into their room.

Wow, that is the first time they actually listened to me, Ariel thought. *They must be clones, because the brothers I know don't listen. Maybe they finally found their conscience.*

Ariel's parents came into the living room. "So what did you guys want to talk to me about?" she asked.

They looked at each other with fear about what she might think in the next five minutes. This conversation was going to hit her hard.

"Ariel, first you have to know that we love you very much," said Ariel's dad.

Ariel was concerned about what they were going to say next.

They sat down and were about to tell her the whole story about the day Ariel had been found. They were going to tell Ariel that she was their god daughter, how her real parents had died, and how they adopted her.

Just as her dad was supposed to speak, there was a loud boom in the building. There was screaming and terror coming from a couple floors below them. "What was that?" The Smiths looked outside the slider door and saw flames and dark smoke coming from two floors down.

Smoke came from every direction, and the air started to turn black. Mr. and Mrs. Smith made all three kids go down the fire escape first. "Go Go now! Get out of here." The fire escape went all the way down to the street so it was a perfect escape plan for a situation like this.

Ariel and her brothers made it down safely. Their parents said that they were going to be right behind them. Once they reached the bottom, Ariel looked up, and all she saw was flames from the eighth floor.

Another loud boom came from the building. This time, the whole building went up in flames.

Ariel was a wreck. She wanted to get in the building and try and save people, but Aaron held her back. "We have to go save them!" she implored. He wasn't going to let her risk her life to go in and try and find their mom and dad. Aaron knew that he would never see his parents again, but Ariel couldn't handle it.

She kicked and screamed trying to get away from Aaron, but eventually she gave up. Her knees fell to the ground, and she cried with Aaron by her side. Then Eric found them and dropped to his knees, weeping about what just happened.

Ariel thought about how they had something very important to tell her, and they didn't get the chance. That made her only more upset, but still she wanted the answers to all of her questions.

She looked around and saw fire trucks swarming the street. Loud sirens wailed as firemen hopped down from their trucks to go to work. The firemen ran into the burning building with bravery and courage. All she could do was stand and wait. There was absolutely nothing she could do, and she felt helpless.

5

HER STORY

Ariel and her brothers survived that terrible fire. Many other people were not so lucky, like their parents. The entire building collapsed to the ground due to the dangerous fire that took place that night.

The fire started on the eighth floor, which was Chelsea's floor. She managed to get out alive with only minor injuries. Chelsea's parents were shocked to find out what had happened while they were away on business, but they were grateful that their daughter was okay.

What was once their home was turned to burnt rubble. The sight was almost unrecognizable, and smoke still filled the air even after the fire was put out.

After having her home destroyed, Ariel and her brothers stayed with their grandmother in Sommerville. She opened her home up for three teenagers and didn't regret it one bit. Some days were harder than others, but she loved having them around the house.

Eventually, Ariel got the story out of her grandmother. It was a story she had been waiting to hear her whole life. It was shocking to Ariel, and she kept replaying it in her head.

The Smiths had adopted Ariel when she was really young. Her

grandmother wanted to tell her the rest of the story about her real parents, but every time, Ariel would cover her ears with a pillow. She didn't want to know why her parents had put her up for adoption. She didn't want to know anything about them.

After hiding out in her room for a while, she wanted to ask her brothers some questions. Ariel then realized that they weren't really her brothers at all. They were simply two boys with whom she lived.

She walked into their room. Aaron was on his laptop, and Eric was reading a book. This was the first time Ariel had ever walked into their room before. Usually, they were the ones who wanted to barge in her room.

Ariel said, "You guys knew?" They both looked up from what they were doing and saw that Ariel was still upset about the recent events. "You both knew, and you didn't tell me!" She stomped her foot into the carpet while making fists.

Eric closed his book and said, "Ariel, Mom and Dad thought it was best for you not to know. They wanted us to stay a family."

There was silence in the room, and Ariel said, "How long have you known?"

Aaron said, "Only a couple years. Ariel, we still love you, and Mom and Dad would want us to stay together."

Ariel said, "Don't you guys realize? They're not even my parents! My real parents are who knows where, and now who I thought were my parents are dead!" She ran out of the room, avoiding crying in front of Aaron and Eric.

Aaron turned to Eric and said, "This is really bad. I knew that she wouldn't take it well. Grandma shouldn't have told her."

Eric said, "She would've found out eventually. At least Grandma didn't tell her everything."

Aaron thought Eric was right, but he hoped that this recent news wouldn't change Ariel's opinion about him.

Ariel hid under her covers for two days straight. She only ate when her grandma brought her food. Aaron was concerned about her and wanted to bring her out of her slump. With warm milk and cookies in hand, Aaron went to cheer Ariel up with her favorite snack. She could never turn down milk and cookies.

Aaron entered her room and sat on the bed. "Ariel, I have your favorite: milk and cookies." Ariel reached out from her blanket, took the cookies off the plate, and slipped back into her blanket cocoon. Aaron could hear her munching on the cookie from under her covers. "Come on, Ariel. You can't stay in here forever. Do you remember that day when we were at the park and were feeding a family of ducks a few years ago?" Ariel said yes and started to slowly come out of her cocoon. "Well, do you remember what Mom said? Families of ducks stick together no matter what. Even though they might not all be family, they love each other and will protect one another."

Ariel remembered her adoptive mom saying that like it was yesterday. Aaron's kind words of encouragement got Ariel out of bed. She decided to start living again and tried to be happy.

Even though Aaron and Eric didn't have the same DNA as Ariel, she still stayed very close with them throughout high school. Every time they got off the bus from school, they raced back to their grandmother's house. Waiting for them was freshly baked cookies right out of the oven. Their grandma spoiled them with love and sweets.

For the last two years of high school, they lived with their grandma. The deal was she would cook them sweets, and they would help her around the house. Ariel was in charge of watering the garden and making sure the bird feeders were full. Aaron would mow the lawn and wash the floors. Eric would do all the laundry. He did not look forward to washing his grandma's old bloomers.

They loved living with their grandma. Sometimes they got on each other's nerves. They got into fights about not doing their homework or not finishing their vegetables at dinner. Sometimes their grandma was harder on them than their parents were, but she did it for a good reason. She loved them with all her heart. She even loved Ariel as a person and accepted her as her own granddaughter.

At first, when her son told her that they were going to welcome Ariel into the family, Grandma had been a little worried. Raising Aaron and Eric together was already a handful. Welcoming a third child into the family was going to cause more stress.

Regina was simply looking out for her son and how much more would be put on his back. Once Ariel started living with her, it was a completely different story. Regina knew that Ariel was not a true Smith, but all that went away when she got to know her.

She and Ariel bonded like every granddaughter and grandmother should. It didn't start out that way, but like every other relationship, it took time.

6

THE LETTER

Two years later, Ariel, Aaron, and Eric had saved up enough money to rent their own apartment off campus. With financial aid paying for their education, they were able to afford their own place and not live in the dormitories. They were all eighteen when they were accepted into the same university. Boston University was where they had wanted to go to since they were young.

For such a long time, Ariel had had no idea what she wanted to do with her life. By the time she was twelve, she had changed her mind several times. She'd wanted to be a princess, a circus performer, a ballerina, a singer, a game show host, a teacher, and even a doctor. With all those things in mind, she decided to go a different route. She decided to major in animation.

She had a love for animated movies, especially Disney movies. She had her own ideas that she wanted to make into reality. Maybe someday she would be a part of making a Disney movie. Who knew where this could take her?

Aaron was on the right path to becoming an NBA player. He got a full scholarship to play for Boston University, still loving the game as much as he had when he was a kid. He was busy with classes all the time, and he couldn't watch or go to as many Celtics games as he would've liked. He made it a tradition to go to a Celtics game every January.

While Aaron complained about how busy he was, Eric was ten times busier. Eric double majored in computer science and engineering. Eric's fist choice was Harvard, but like everything else, Aaron got his wish and made Eric apply to Boston University. They had to go to the same university or else they wouldn't survive without each other. They were inseparable like most twins were. Even though Boston University wasn't his first choice, Eric was glad that Aaron and Ariel were going to be with him.

It was a snowy day in Boston, and Ariel was walking back from a class. She'd had an awful week. She hadn't done so well on her big project, and her grandmother had just passed away from old age, at ninety. Also, it was nearing the anniversary her adoptive parents' death, and so she was very emotional.

When she walked in her apartment, she quickly closed the door so no cold air would come through the door. She let out a sigh and took off her scarf. She then took off her coat and hat. Her boots were covered in snow, and so she left them by the heater to let them dry. She went into the kitchen to make some hot cocoa to warm up.

When she was in the middle of making her hot cocoa, she stared outside the window and watched the snow fall. Many thoughts went through her head. She was about ready to burst, and then she said, "That's it—I can't take it anymore! I have to know!" She ran upstairs to her bedroom, leaving her hot cocoa on the coffee table.

She opened her desk draw and dug underneath old notebooks until she found a letter. She held the letter in her hand and started to cry. Then she held the letter close to her heart and walked back downstairs. She sat on the couch with her cocoa and was ready to open it.

Before Mr. and Mrs. Smith had died, they'd written a letter to each of their kids. Aaron and Eric had already opened their letters the minute they got them. Their parents had opened up a safe deposit box for the letters. Ariel always wanted to open hers, but she didn't have the guts to do it. Ariel was afraid to reveal more about herself or her parents. She wanted to get some closure but feared that this letter would be too much to bear. She took a deep breath and started opening the side of the envelope.

Dear Ariel,

If you are reading this, that means we have gone to a better place. We know you are probably still hurting, but think of the happy memories that we've had together instead of grieving. We decided to write you this letter because when we did die, we didn't want you to feel like we didn't treat you like one of our own. Even though Aaron and Eric are still probably troublemakers, we can say that you were our most well-behaved child.

Now, since you're reading this, you probably want find out more about your real parents. Ariel, please prepare yourself, because this might come to a bit of a shock. Please promise you won't be angry with us keeping this secret from you. We wanted you to live a happy healthy life.

Back when your father was named detective and Aaron and Eric were just born, we found you. Your father had to do an investigation at a crime scene. We knew your parents, Ariel. We'd known them since high school. When your mom had you, your dad surprised her by purchasing a new house on Elm Street. It was an up-and-coming neighborhood, perfect for a young couple and a baby. They were the very first house on the street. Everything went great

for a while. Your parents loved you so much, Ariel—
you have to know that. I'm sure they're looking down
on you and watching over you this very second. Your
parents' names were Amy and Sean. Ariel, you have
the same qualities as your mother. You have her eyes
and her personality. Your parents never would've given
you up for anything in the whole world.

Ariel, your birth parents were murdered in the
fall of 1999. Your father was the detective who was
sent to the address. He didn't know that Amy and
Sean were killed until he saw them on the ground.
Your father stuck around to find some more evidence,
and he wasn't going to leave until he found you. He
heard crying from the upstairs closet. Who knows
what you heard or saw? You couldn't have remembered
it anyway, because you were so young.

You weren't put into foster care because we were
your godparents. Amy and Sean made sure that if
anything happened to them, we would be the ones to
raise you. Please forgive us for not telling you sooner.
The case was closed up a long time ago. The killer was
never arrested, and we wanted justice for you, but there
wasn't any found. There was no prime suspect in the
case. We wanted to tell you, but you were too young
to understand at the time we wrote this. We thought
writing a letter would be best. Also, there is a little
photo album at the back of this letter to show you what
your parents looked like, and to go down memory lane
when we found you.

Ariel, we love you so very much, and we will be
watching over you every step of the way. We hope that
you live your life to the fullest, and that you always
love your friends and family. You'll never know the

last time you're going to see them, or the last time you give them a hug. Those are precious moments that you need to hold on to. Don't take them for granted, and don't forget them.

If you're still looking for answers, you can go to your old house, where we found you. The address is 1 Elm Street in Dorchester. You would always ask us, "Why does that big, blue house have boards on the windows?" when we would go to the park. We would make up a story, but that was the house where Amy and Sean were killed. They boarded up the place so no one would go inside anymore. It probably is still like that today, because it was filed as an unsolved case. The police department kept the case open for years, but they eventually gave up. It's been so many years that the only way they can reopen the case is if they find any new evidence that could point to the killer. If they did find something, it would be a miracle, but I highly doubt it, my dear.

Promise us you'll be good, and try to keep Aaron and Eric in line—as much as you can, at least. We love you, Ariel.

Your godparents,
Allison and David

Ariel couldn't believe what she had just read. She wanted to cry and scream at the same time. She sat up on her couch to look outside. She wanted to go to Elm Street and look at the house she could've grown up in. *No wonder I didn't look like them. My gut always told me that I wasn't a Smith.*

She couldn't go today; the snowstorm was getting worse, and the power could possibly go out. She would have to wait until the snow stopped. She had never wanted the snow to stop so much in her life.

She saw the photo album hanging on the bottom of the letter. The album was so small she could fit it in her pocket. Clear plastic covered the pictures. She remembered what the letter said. She didn't want to see her real parents in those pictures. She ripped the album into tiny pieces and threw it in the trash can in the kitchen. Then she jumped back onto the couch, feeling angry.

Who would want to murder such innocent people? I can't even imagine the pain they went through. Throwing those pictures away was for the best because they were only going to cause Ariel more pain regarding what could've been.

Elm Street wasn't too far from campus. Ariel had a million things on her mind. She was so grateful that her godparents had taken her in. *What would've happened to me if they didn't take me?* Ariel thought. She would've grown up in foster care, waiting to be adopted by some stranger, and she never would've found out the truth about her real parents.

She lay on the couch with her cocoa, waiting for the snow to stop falling. She checked the forecast on her phone; it said that the snow wasn't going to stop for a while. She waited for Aaron and Eric to come home. *They shouldn't be out in this terrible weather.* Ariel needed a hug from them more than anything right now.

A few hours later, Aaron and Eric walked back from class. Eric had a lab to do, and Aaron had basketball practice with his team. They came through the door with laughter and comedy like they always did, followed by a gust of cold, winter air. Eric shut the door behind them, and they turned around. Then they realized that Ariel was crying on the couch.

Ariel was curled up in a blanket on the couch, a pillow underneath her head. The side of the pillow was wet from her tears.

Aaron ran over to her quickly, sat down next to her, and put a hand on her shoulder. "Ariel, what's wrong?" Eric stood a few feet away, assessing the situation. He tried to figure out why she was crying. Numerous events had happened in their lives, and Ariel seemed to be the most emotional when it came to certain news.

Ariel took out her opened letter from underneath her blanket and gave it to Aaron. She had stuffed the letter back into the ripped envelope. They could tell that the letter had been opened, and that was what made Ariel so upset. Aaron said, "You finally opened your letter."

Ariel pulled the blanket over her face and said, "Yes." Then she let out a whimper.

Aaron put the letter on the coffee table and let out a sigh after reading it. He couldn't imagine what was going through her mind right now. *Ariel has gone through so much and has been through so much pain.* "Is there anything I can do for you?"

Ariel shook her head side to side. A moment passed by. "Can I just have a hug? Can you guys come with me to Elm Street?" Ariel face was shiny due do her crying, and she wrapped her arms around Aaron's strong back. Aaron didn't ask any questions and said yes to every one of her questions.

Eric grabbed the letter from the coffee table and read it for himself. He too felt emotion for Ariel, but he was glad that he didn't have to pretend to not know anything anymore. Ariel finally knew everything about her real parents and how they'd died. For a moment, Aaron was the only one comforting Ariel, but then Eric came in and joined the hug. Eric thought hugs were overrated.

Aaron whispered to Ariel, "Everything is going to be okay. I'm here. It's okay, Ariel."

The wounds of their parents passing were still very fresh. There wouldn't be a day that went by that Aaron and Eric wouldn't think of them. Their conscience was now completely clear, now that Ariel finally knew the whole truth.

7

SEEING RED

Finally the storm passed, and Eric informed them that there was five feet of snow on the porch. Cold winter air blew in every direction, and icicles hung from the shingles of houses. Today was the day Ariel was going to visit the house she would've grown up in, where her parents had been killed and where David Smith had found Ariel when she was a toddler. Aaron gladly paid for the Uber to take them to Elm Street. Ariel tried to reason with him, saying that they should split it, but he insisted.

She didn't care that it was freezing cold outside. After living in Boston all her life, she'd was adjusted to the cold. Ariel wanted to see the house for herself and hoped to get some closure. She felt that there would be no more pain from this day forward, if she could achieve the task of seeing the crime scene.

When the Uber dropped them off, Ariel slowly walked down the driveway. Because it had snowed yesterday, everything was like an ice rink. Aaron was right behind her, ready to catch her if she fell. Eric started to get jealous of how Aaron was treating Ariel lately, waiting on her hand and foot.

Last night, Aaron had been by her side all night. He did whatever she told him to do. He made her dinner and dessert to try to make her feel better. For dessert, he made her chocolate chip cookies. They were out of milk, and so he went outside in the blizzard to get some milk. It was meant to help her take her mind off of things. Aaron had never done that much for anyone before.

Aaron had been a light in darkness to Ariel. At other times, he had to be the one to take care of her, the shoulder to cry on. There was only one person in the entire world that made Aaron smile. He smiled a lot normally, but he smiled a different way when he talked to Ariel. When Aaron smiled and looked at Ariel, a dense dimple appeared in his right cheek. He only had one dimple, and it was on the right side of his face. Ariel was the only person who brought that out of him.

In the Uber car, Ariel sat in the back between Aaron and Eric. She was sitting in between them and felt like she was squished like a sandwich. Her ears were at their shoulder level.

Ariel let out a sigh and looked up at them both. They smiled down at her. Then they all broke out laughing in the back seat of the cab. The cab driver thought they were crazy for laughing so much.

Aaron and Eric couldn't even cross their legs. When they tried, they ended up squishing Ariel even more. Ariel felt like she was about to pop like a balloon, but they laughed it off. They kept goofing off while the cab driver kept doing his job. They acted like their happy-go-lucky selves, which they hadn't done that for a while. They were trying to make this occasion a little bearable for Ariel, acting like nothing had gone wrong over the years.

Finally, the Uber stopped, and the driver said, "One Elm Street," in his Spanish accent.

Aaron looked down at Ariel and said, "You ready?" Ariel nodded while she put on her gloves.

Aaron opened the door and stepped out. His eyes concentrated on the house. While looking at the house, he kept the door open for Ariel to come out. The cold winter breeze made his scarf, which was wrapped around his neck, blow east. When Ariel got out of the Uber, she stared at the house. Then Eric got out of the Uber and shut the door. The Uber car drove off.

They stood in the cold and looked at the house. Aaron was on one side and Eric was on the other, with Ariel in the middle.

Three feet of snow was on top of the roof, and icicles hung from the gutters. Ariel looked at the house she was supposed to grow up in, seeing it for the first time. The color of the house was dark blue. All of the windows and doors were boarded up by wood. Some of the wood on the house was falling off. Even the dark blue paint of the house was fading. She took a deep breath and started to walk towards the house.

She looked to her left and saw that it had snowed so much last night that just the very top of the mailbox was visible. It was black, and the red flag on the side had a sheet of ice covering it, but she could still see the bright color red through that sheet of ice.

They dredged through the snow to get to the porch. Ariel had basically swum through the snow, and it was up past her waist; Aaron and Eric merely had to high-step through the snow.

Ariel thought about what if she'd actually grown up in this house. What if so many events hadn't happened? She could see herself playing on the front lawn. She saw herself playing on the front porch with her toys. She tried to imagine what the house would be like if it was kept up all these years, if it hadn't been condemned. She saw a happy life of what could've been.

Ariel envisioned a summer day in July. The sun was shining bright, and there wasn't a cloud in the sky. The flower beds in front of the house were being blown by a gentle breeze. The sun was shining bright, followed by laughter and happiness; it was Ariel. She was flying her kite through the air. She imagined her younger self being joyful and happy. Her blonde hair blew through the humid air, and she smiled up at her kite as she ran around the front yard.

She looked across the yard and saw a younger version of Aaron and Eric flying their kites too. They ran through the wind, heading toward Ariel while laughing and screaming. Then they started chasing Ariel, and so she started to run with her kite. They ran into the backyard and out to the front yard again. They kept running in circles around the house.

In her vision, when Ariel ran past the porch, she glanced over to Allison and David, her godparents. They were also with Ariel's real parents. They sat together at a table drinking lemonade and having a good time. They were laughing and telling old stories. Ariel wanted it to be real more than anything in the whole world.

Back in reality, snowflakes were blowing off the trees and onto Ariel's face. She was only envisioning what could've been her happy childhood with her parents in it. Everything would've been perfect, and she wanted that to be her childhood. Sadly, it wasn't.

Then she remembered that Allison and David had given her a happy childhood. She forgot how much they loved her and cherished her. She had a pretty good childhood after all. She simply hadn't appreciated as much as she should have at the time.

Ariel finally reached the porch, which was submerged in snow. It was only up to her calves though, so it was easier to walk. With every step she took, the boards creaked, and she was afraid that she would fall through the porch. She looked at the front door, which was boarded up with three-inch-thick boards that were bolted on the door frame.

Aaron and Eric were secretly scared of seeing this place in person. Their parents had told them that this house was haunted, but they hadn't believed them. What haunted house gets condemned, anyway? They drove by Elm constantly when they went to the park, which was just a few streets down. They had gone to the park almost every day when they were young.

Ariel gazed at the bottom of the door and realized that there was an opening at the bottom of the door. Her first instinct was to crawl into the hole because she was the only one who could fit through there. She bent down to see if the hole could take her inside, and she could see the carpet inside the house through the small opening. She crouched down and started to crawl on her hands and knees to go through the hole. She felt the cold frozen snow through her jeans when she bent down on all fours.

Aaron tried to grab her and said, "Ariel wait!" He grabbed her arm.

Ariel looked back and said, "What do you think I'm doing? I'm finally getting the answers I've wanted since I was young. Once I get inside, I'll figure out a way to let you guys in."

Aaron let go of her, and she proceeded into the house. It was a tight fit, but she pushed her tiny waist through that hole of the door. Once she got through the hole, she stood up and brushed the snow off her legs. She looked around, and it still looked like a crime scene. White sheets covered the furniture in the living room. It appeared that the sheets hadn't been touched in years because she could see layers of dust resting on them. She looked down at the carpet in the living room and saw something rather disturbing.

In the carpet of the living room were two huge stains of dried blood from the victims many years ago. Ariel knew that it was from eighteen years ago. She let out a gasp at realizing that it was her mom's and dad's blood.

She tried to not pay attention to the blood stains on the carpet, and her eyes wondered to the corner of the room. There was a little brown end table that had been tipped over. A vintage phone and a recording machine had been knocked off the table. The phone was a few feet from where the second blood stain was in the carpet.

Then she looked back down at the first blood stain she saw, which was more in the center of the room. She thought that her parents hadn't known the murderer was still in the home, and her mother or father had proceeded to call for help, but obviously that hadn't worked out for them. She thought about the pain they must have endured while they were suffering.

Ariel heard Aaron say outside, "Ariel you okay in there?"

She wiped a tear off her face and said, "Yeah, I'm fine." Then she turned around to see the yellow police tape in the corner of the room, covered in dust. Ariel unlocked the door and tried to open it. The boards were bolted into the door frame, blocking them from getting inside. Ariel felt a gust of cold winter air blowing into the house. She could only see Aaron and Eric through the small cracks of the boards. "Is there any way you can break down the boards?" Ariel thought for a moment that they could be arrested for trespassing, but it was an old crime scene that had been closed over a decade ago. There shouldn't be any problems.

Aaron placed his hand on one of the boards and pulled it. It turned out they were all rotted. He looked at Eric with a funny face. "Wish we'd known this earlier so we wouldn't be out here shivering to death." They tore the boards apart. Once they got in the house, Ariel shut the door. It wasn't that much warmer inside the house because of the hole at the bottom of the door.

Eric said, "We're almost better off on the porch. It's freezing in here. I can see my breath." Then they started looking around.

Aaron walked into what appeared like a dining room. A white sheet covered what looked like a long table and chairs. He noticed the phone and table tipped over before entering the dining room. In the room to the right was a hutch hanging on the wall. Inside was some very expensive-looking china.

Ariel and Eric proceeded to the center of the room. Sheets covered what it looked like to be two big couches and a small table. This room seemed to be the living room. Eric then saw the blood stains on the carpet. He figured that was how Ariel's parents had died, from loss of blood due to the severe wounds.

The ceilings were really high. It was a pretty big house, and it was a great house to start a family. Ariel kept creeping around the massive blood stains in the carpet. At one point, she stepped on the blood stain and felt as if she had stepped on her parents' corpses. Then something caught her eye.

Eric wasn't that impressed. He thought that he would see more damage to the house or more of a crime scene. He said, "Well, Ariel, I have a paper to write."

Really? Not even concerned about me and why he was there in the first place, she thought.

He looked at Ariel. She stared at the picture frame on the wall. Eric was concerned about what she was looking at in the picture, and so he walked over to her. He stood next to her, and his eyes widened in surprise. He yelled, "Aaron, get in here!" Within a few seconds, Aaron joined them. They all stared at the picture on the wall.

Ariel brushed off the dust and cobwebs to get a better view of the picture. Tears filled her eyes once again. She finally said, "That's me when I was a baby." The picture was in a white frame with layers of dust on it. In the picture was a baby.

Aaron said, "Mom and Dad kept that picture of you in their dresser draw. This must really be Amy and Sean's house, then."

A few feet from that picture was another on the wall. This one had more people in it. It was like a collage, and it was handmade by someone very crafty.

There were four different pictures in that one frame. The first picture was Ariel when she was just born. The next picture was Ariel's mom holding her in a hospital bed. She had a smile on her face while she held her baby daughter. Ariel could see why her godparents had said that she looked like her mom. Ariel saw herself in that picture when she looked at her mom.

The picture on the lower left was a picture of Ariel's parents and her godparents when they were younger. The picture was taken when they were in college together. The last picture on the lower right was Ariel, Aaron, and Eric when they were first born.

Ariel's mom had glued the pictures together to make it look like one big picture. They looked like they were about a day old in all of their pictures. In those picture frames, Ariel felt the happiest she had ever been in a long time. She had never seen these pictures before, and neither had Aaron or Eric. She was truly touched at how much her parents loved her. She didn't remember them, but she knew that they loved her very much. Tears were in her eyes, but a big smile was on her face.

Aaron comforted her by telling her stories about their mom and dad, and how much they'd loved her too. Meanwhile, Eric was disgusted by all the touching and heartfelt moments.

Ariel hugged Aaron, who looked to Eric with his eyes, saying, *That conversation that we just had on the porch stays between us.*

Eric got the message by reading his facial expressions, and he decided to keep quiet. Eric nodded. Most of the time, Eric agreed with Aaron to avoid having an argument.

8

NOT BY BLOOD

When Ariel went through the hole in the door, Aaron and Eric were left all alone. Eric said, "Okay let's just cut to the chase, Aaron."

Aaron looked oddly at Eric like he didn't know what he was talking about, but he did know. "There's nothing to talk about, Eric, so just drop it!"

Eric wasn't going to let this one go. "You can't keep hiding this, Aaron. You need to tell Ariel how you really feel about her. You can't keep acting like this."

Aaron thought on it for a second before he opened his mouth. "What am I supposed to say? 'Ariel, I know we're not really related anymore, so I'm telling you that I'm in love with you'?"

"Please, Aaron. Ever since the day Mom and Dad told us that Ariel was adopted, you have been obsessing about her. You need to stop this madness, or you might lose her."

"Eric, I can't do that, even though we're not family by blood. I still consider her my best friend in the whole world. We grew up together! I can't ruin what we have. What if she doesn't feel the same way about me? Then it will be awkward forever."

Eric thought about Aaron's situation and tried to come up with an idea to help him. Then they heard Ariel inside, gasping as if she was scared.

Inside the house, Aaron was still hugging Ariel. Eric understood what Aaron was trying to tell him, by not saying anything in front of Ariel. Eric went back in his mind when they were fifteen, when they would spy on Ariel all the time.

The main reason Aaron and Eric would spy on Ariel was because Aaron had a massive crush on Ariel. Ever since Aaron had found out that Ariel wasn't really her sister, he couldn't control his feelings for her, Like a bacon cheeseburger, it was very hard to resist.

Even when Eric said to Ariel, "I know who has a crush on you," She didn't believe anyone would ever have a crush on her. Little did she know that her crush's bedroom was right across from hers.

Several times Aaron tried to have Ariel see that he liked her, but she thought he simply wasn't being rotten for once. Aaron tried to show a different side of himself to her, but she didn't understand why he would be so nice to her.

Aaron wanted to have a relationship with Ariel, but he feared that if he told her how he really felt, it could ruin their friendship forever.

After Ariel stopped looking at the pictures on the wall, she wanted to see the rest of the house. When she finished looking through the first floor, she wanted to inspect the second floor. At the bottom of the stairs, she recalled the letter her godparents have given her. It said that David had found Ariel in a closet. She went up the stairs.

First, she went into a room with pink painted walls. She looked underneath the sheets that were covering the furniture. There was a crib and small dresser, with teddy bears all around the room. It was Ariel's nursery, which she'd lived in for only a short period of time. Even though pink wasn't her favorite color, Ariel still liked the room.

Then Ariel walked into her parents' bedroom. There was a king-size bed with curtains made of silk. She walked into the center of the room to find a half-opened closet. She thought that this was the closet in which her godfather found her. If he didn't hear her screaming then, Ariel probably would've died from starvation or dehydration.

Ariel kept looking around the room, thinking about what had happened and why her parents had put her in that closet. Then she started thinking about what might have actually happened.

On that cold fall night, Ariel's mom was getting ready to put her to sleep. She held her child in her arms and gave her a bottle. She rocked her child to sleep in her arms so that she too could get some needed sleep. She always gave her a bottle before bed. Ariel's dad was lying in the bed reading a book, and suddenly he heard a loud bang.

"Amy, did you hear that?" It came from downstairs.

Amy looked up from Ariel in shock and said, "Yeah. Go check it out." Sean followed his wife's orders and decided to go downstairs to investigate.

A few minutes went by, and Amy was concerned about what her husband was doing. With Ariel in her arms, she walked downstairs. She peeked around the corner and saw an intruder in the living room. Sean was unaware of where he was. The intruder lifted up his knife and stabbed Sean in his back. The knife entered through his back and came out the front of his body.

Amy was so frightened that she almost dropped Ariel. She ran upstairs without looking back, frantically searching for a place to hide. She found a place for Ariel. In her bedroom closet, she laid down Ariel, who was swaddled in her blanket. Amy closed the door and raced downstairs to the phone in the living room to call 911. Her hands were shaking so quickly that it was hard for her to dial the three numbers.

She didn't know that the intruder was still in the house. The operator said, "This is 911, what's your emergency?" Before Amy could say anything else, she was stabbed in the stomach. The suspect fled the scene and went out the front door. Amy collapsed, lying there next to her husband, who was already dead.

Ariel was left in that closet for only a couple of minutes until Mr. Smith found her. It was such a tragedy. And to think that the killer was never caught.

Back to reality, Ariel wanted to see if there was anything left of her parents' belongings. She slammed open the other side of the closet to find the whole closet completely empty. Ariel was mad that there was nothing left of her parents besides the pictures downstairs hanging on the wall. The police had cleaned out all of their belongings. She shook her head and frowned.

Ariel ripped off the white sheets on the dressers and pulled out all the drawers. There was nothing inside but dust and cobwebs. Then she slammed all of them shut. She started searching the whole house, stomping her feet with every step she took.

"Hey, Ariel, are you okay?" Aaron said from the bottom of the stairs.

Ariel ran down the stairs. "They took everything! There's got to be something here!" she mumbled in distress.

Aaron and Eric weren't sure what they'd just heard.

Eric said, "What?"

She ran past them. "There's got to be something here. Anything! Why isn't anything here?" She became violent and started banging her feet and punching the wall.

Aaron immediately tried to stop her. "Hey! Hey, stop it!" He tried to put his arms around her, but she ran away from him. "Stop, Ariel. Just stop!"

She cried, "No! why? They took everything away, like they didn't even exist!"

Ariel finally calmed down, but she was still angry about the police taking all of their belongings. It was as if they didn't live here anymore. The police took everything like they were nothing, like they weren't even real. They took everything and probably threw it away.

Aaron felt Ariel's pain and how crushed she was.

She thought that by coming here, she would found something that was her parents, so that she would have some closure. Aaron and Eric never really saw her express her feelings like that before, but today she couldn't keep it inside anymore.

She apologized to Aaron and Eric for her behavior. It was getting pretty late, and so they wanted to head back to the apartment. Aaron and Eric waited for Ariel to spend some time alone in her parents' house.

She walked around in the dining room, picturing what her life could've been like. Then she spotted the collage picture on the wall once again. She loved that picture on the wall, even though an hour ago she hadn't known it existed. The police department cleaned everything out except the furniture and the pictures on the wall. Also, the china collection in the dining room was still here. All was handed over to private investigators to see if there was any evidence that connected to the case. She took one last look and then shut the door behind her. She knew her brothers were outside waiting for her.

A strong gust of wind blew as she shut the door. She then saw the Uber waiting for her on the street, with Aaron holding the door open for her. After everything she'd done today, he was such a gentleman to her. No one had ever treated Ariel so nicely. it made her heart feel good inside.

9

SURPRISE

Three years later, it was the eve of Ariel's twenty-first birthday. It was almost midnight, and Ariel was working on a paper that was due Monday morning. It was a paper she should've started earlier, but she was a master procrastinator. *Why did I wait to start this until now? Stupid brain! Stupid me!*

When the clock struck midnight, Ariel was in for a very special birthday. She was typing on her laptop, and then suddenly Aaron and Eric burst through the door with noisemakers and party hats. They started singing happy birthday to her, even though she hated being sung to.

They danced around her merrily. Ariel sat in her computer chair with her arms crossed and a smile on her face, trying not to laugh, but she couldn't hold it. During their singing, Aaron put a party hat on Ariel's head. She started laughing, and then she realized they had their presents behind them in the hallway. *Why couldn't this all wait until morning?* she thought.

Aaron said, "We couldn't wait to give you your presents," as he grabbed them from the hallway.

Ariel couldn't believe how awesome Aaron and Eric were, but

she couldn't stand that they had to do this every year at the time the clock struck twelve. "Seriously, you guys couldn't wait until morning?"

Eric said, "Look at your clock. It says a.m., doesn't it?"

Ariel smiled and said to herself, *Eric is right. Technically, it is morning.* She probably wouldn't wake up until tomorrow afternoon, anyway.

Aaron got her a limited edition Larry Bird jersey. Eric made her an alarm clock out of an old clock so that he wouldn't have to be the one to wake her up in the morning. Ariel had an alarm on her phone but chose to never use it. Eric was the one who made sure that she wasn't late for her morning classes. Now, he could sleep in when he didn't have classes, and she could get woken up by herself.

Ariel wasn't really a morning person. Every morning she woke up to go to class, she found herself falling asleep.

Eric would go back to sleep after he woke up Ariel. Eric thought that Ariel was getting older, and he would tease her about it every year on her birthday. Little did Ariel know that Aaron and Eric had big plans for her this year. It was a birthday that she would never forget.

Luckily, Ariel's birthday was on a Saturday, and so she didn't have any classes. Ariel's new alarm clock went off at 9:00 a.m. As a joke, Eric had set it to get her up for her special breakfast, and to make sure she didn't miss her big day.

She awoke feeling as if she'd just fallen asleep. She looked right, still resting her head on her pillow, and saw on her desk was Eric's alarm clock. She thought it would turn off by itself, but it kept making an annoying, bell-ringing noise. She flipped the covers off her bed and walked over to the alarm clock. She put her hand on the top of the clock, shutting it off. She put it back down on her desk, before hearing a loud bang coming from downstairs.

When she walked downstairs, she could smell an aroma coming from the kitchen. She was concerned that they would burn down the house from cooking, and so she rushed to the kitchen. She saw them cooking side by side. On the table was a buffet of food. She was almost taken aback by what she saw and thought she was still dreaming. "Is all of this for me?"

Aaron turned around and said, "There's the birthday girl!" He smiled, and the dimple popped up. "Don't worry about a thing. We'll take care of everything."

Ariel thought that something wasn't right. Every time they tried to cook something, they always ended up burning it, or it tasted awful. "How'd did you guys learn how to cook? You both can't boil water."

Eric said, "Yeah, we just learned how to read cookbooks." Then he lifted up the cookbook he was using to make all of the breakfast food.

She went back in her mind about how they'd both tried to make Mom pancakes for Mother's Day. It had been a complete disaster. Instead of waking up to fresh, warm pancakes, she'd woken up to a smoke-filled kitchen and severely burnt pancakes.

Ariel said, "That's great, guys, but you don't have to do this all for me."

Aaron was shocked at her unselfishness and said, "Yes, we do— and don't you lift a finger. We've got it all covered." They insisted on giving her a perfect birthday, and it started with the perfect breakfast.

They made her chocolate chip pancakes, scrambled eggs, fresh muffins, and bacon. Aaron poured her a cup of coffee and made freshly squeezed orange juice. Ariel hadn't really had a sweet sixteen birthday party, and so they wanted to make this milestone birthday extra special.

After Ariel feasted on her birthday breakfast, Aaron entered the kitchen with something behind his back.

"Oh, my god. I'm never eating again," she said. "I feel like two hundred pounds."

"Nonsense. You still look beautiful, Ariel," Aaron replied. Clearly he had another present of some sort, because he had a huge smile on his face. His dimple was still gleaming, excited to see Ariel's reaction to his next gift. His attractive and dazzling smile was always a dead giveaway.

Aaron sat next to Ariel at the table. "Remember the old apartment building that we used to live in? The one where Mom and Dad died?"

Ariel went back in her head, thinking about that horrible day. She nodded.

"Well, after it burned to the ground, Eric and I went through the wreckage. I don't know how, but remember that bucket list you made when you were nine? You kept it in your desk drawer for years. I don't know how, but it survived the fire."

Ariel's desk was made out of iron, and somehow it had fallen to the bottom of the building when it was collapsing from the fire. The desk sealed everything inside the drawer, and everything was unharmed inside: her bucket list, and a bracelet she'd made with blue and red pearls. Ariel looked at the bracelet she'd made over a decade ago. She looked at how small it appeared, and how it didn't fit her anymore.

Aaron then pulled out the bucket list from behind his back and gave it to Ariel. Written in purple marker was Ariel's bucket list before she turned twenty-one. She gasped at seeing it, wondering how on earth it had survived the fire in the apartment building. She thought she would never see it again. Even though she was turning twenty-one today, she had never done any of these activities.

"Wait, you've kept this for all this time, and you never gave it me?"

Aaron and Eric looked at each other at the same time. Eric said, "Well, today we were going to check off everything that bucket list."

Ariel jumped from her chair and said, "Shut up! Really? All

right, I'll go get ready." She ran upstairs to get ready for the best birthday ever, and possibly the best day of her life.

Aaron and Eric thought that they should get the best friend award, if there was such a thing. They felt pretty proud of themselves.

To Do Before You're Twenty-one

1. Skydiving
2. Horseback riding
3. Go to a psychic
4. Ice skating
5. Rock climbing
6. Make your own pizza
7. Live life to the fullest

Even though there were only seven things on her bucket list, it was the seven things younger Ariel had promised herself that she would do a long time ago. There were a lot of interesting things and exciting events she had done in her life, but she hadn't done any of these activities. She was always too afraid to attempt them. Now, her mind was in a healthy place, and she was ready to achieve them.

The first activity on her list was skydiving. Ariel was now adventurous, especially when it came to roller coasters. She loved feeling the rush of going through the air. She thought that she would love sky diving too. She also wanted to fly around like Iron Man.

Aaron and Eric took her to the nearest outdoor skydiving facility, where they would take people up in planes. Aaron's first idea was to buy Ariel her own plane, but Eric convinced him to take her to a skydiving facility instead. Aaron always wanted to go the extra step and go over the top for her.

Once Ariel jumped out of that plane, she immediately felt like she was flying through the air. She looked down and could see that she was flying above the whole world. Everything looked small when she was up here. She looked up to see her brothers falling right behind her. Once they got closer to the ground, they pulled their parachutes and landed gently on the ground. It was the most amazing thing Ariel had ever experienced.

Aaron looked at her, smiling from ear to ear. He couldn't stop laughing at how she kept saying, "I can't believe that just happened! I was flying! I was just flying!"

Next, Ariel wanted to ride a horse. When she was younger, she was a little scared of horses. It was probably because of their massive size, and they had big, strong legs. That was why she'd put it on her bucket list, hoping one day she would get over her fear. Eric thought it was interesting that she wasn't afraid of roller coasters, but she was afraid of horses.

Ariel, Aaron, and Eric went on a beautiful horseback ride in a massive field filled with wildflowers. Ariel liked the horse she rode; her name was Sierra. She was a beautiful brown horse with white socks. After the ride, Ariel no longer feared horses, and she felt more connected with them. She wasn't a bit scared of them anymore. She was glad that she got to spend time with one of God's creatures.

After the horses, they went back to campus to get a reading from a psychic. Ariel was rather excited for this activity because she was eager to find out what might come along in her future. Madam Fiona said that Ariel had a very bright future, and she had a lot to look forward to in life. Madam Fiona didn't exactly tell her what it was she had to look forward to; she wanted to keep her surprised.

Ice skating was never really Ariel's forte, but she was eager to learn. When she was younger, she'd hated it because she kept falling down. She had really weak ankles and was afraid that she would hurt herself. Aaron was by her side and guided her around the ice rink until she got the hang of it. After a few hours of trying, she finally made it around the whole ring once without falling at all. Aaron watched her in the middle of the rink.

After skating, they went to a fun gymnasium. There weren't any rocky mountains nearby, and so they decided to climb indoors. It wasn't the real thing, but it was good enough for Ariel. It was one more fun activity after the next, but the day wasn't over yet. Ariel was getting exhausted by everything they did in one day. Aaron kept pulling her along. She went along with it because she knew it was going to be worth it.

After an exciting day, everyone was mighty hungry. Aaron's friend Joe worked at a pizza place, and that was where Ariel made her own pizza. Joe's family owned the pizza place, and luckily they weren't very busy at the time. Joe took time out of his day to show Ariel how to make her own pizza. After she made her own pizza, she put it into the oven and then ate it. It didn't really taste like a regular pizza would taste, but it was still pretty yummy. Everything tastes different, especially when you try to succeed in making it yourself.

With all that had happened that day, Ariel forgot one more thing that was on her bucket list: "Live life to the fullest." From that day on, she did. It was the best birthday she could ever ask for. Little did she know that the day wasn't over yet.

Aaron and Eric had one last surprise for her. This was a real surprise Ariel never saw coming. Once they got back to their apartment, they told Ariel to get all dolled up for a night on the city. Ariel was curious about what they had planned for her, and so she did as they asked. They rushed upstairs to put something on party material.

Aaron smiled while watching Ariel run upstairs excited. It was almost like she hadn't gone out to do anything before. He then tried to envision what her reaction would be after seeing what else he and his brother had planned for her.

10

THE RED DRESS

Ariel had no idea where they were going to take her, and so she decided to go all out. If someone gave her permission to wear the most extravagant thing she owned, she was going to get dressed up for whatever this occasion was going to be. She hoped they wouldn't take her bowling or somewhere they wanted to go. Then she would look all out of sorts!

She pulled a beautiful red dress from her closet. It was classy and had a split down the side, showing a little leg. At only five feet tall, Ariel loved wearing high heels because she felt like a giant for a day. She had a gold pair of stilettos, which she decided to wear. To match, she wore gold hoop earrings and a gold bracelet. Then she put her hair up in a braided bun and was ready to go.

It seemed like she got ready quickly in her head, but she looked at the time on her phone: she'd been getting ready for two hours. Wherever Aaron and Eric were taking her, she hoped it was worth it. *They have been just full of surprises today.*

She put on a lot of makeup to cover her freckles, as well as mascara to make her eyelashes appear longer. She felt good about herself and the way her body looked in that red dress.

Her legs looked stunning in her shoes, with the dress flowing down to the bottom. The split on her dress went up to the middle of her thigh, and there was one shoulder strap on the dress; the other shoulder was exposed. She raised her shoulders up and down, breathing while still looking in her mirror. Ariel was very uncomfortable in her dress. *They couldn't have just asked me to wear jeans and a sweater instead?* she thought.

"Hey, Ariel, you ready?" Aaron yelled from downstairs.

Ariel said, "I'm coming!" She grabbed her coat and went downstairs, hoping she wouldn't trip in her freakishly tall shoes.

When she walked down the stairs, she grabbed the railing so she wouldn't fall. She saw Aaron and Eric waiting at the bottom of the stairs. Aaron gazed at her beauty; she didn't dress up that much. Even though he saw her when she wasn't dressed up, he still saw the beauty in her soul.

She stopped in the middle of the stairs and said, "What? Do I look okay?"

Aaron and Eric looked at each other and laughed slightly. They could tell that she wasn't comfortable in her dress. She probably would've preferred going in sweatpants and a T-shirt. Aaron and Ariel locked eyes from a distance.

Aaron said, "You look perfect." She smiled at Aaron's kind words and hugged them both when she got to the bottom of the stairs. When she did, Aaron smiled at smelling the slightest hint of her perfume.

Even though Ariel wore heels, she was still a lot shorter than them. Ariel didn't seem to mind, but she loved being five inches taller every once in a while. They left to take Ariel to her final surprise of the day.

Ariel had no idea where they were taking her. She was excited and scared, but she was also curious about what else they had up their sleeves.

Aaron and Eric were planning to take Ariel to her favorite restaurant in Boston. She also didn't know that there was going to be a full house of people waiting there for her. Aaron and Eric had planned this surprise party to top off the whole day. It was going to be hard, but like always, Aaron came up with a brilliant idea regarding how to do it.

Before Aaron went in the car to leave, he called one of his friends. Eric and Ariel were waiting in the car for him, and he said he had to go to the bathroom. "Is everything all set up for tonight? Okay, great. We'll be there in twenty minutes." Then he ended his call and went outside.

Once they parked the car, they walked down the street to the restaurant. Ariel's head turned as she thought about where they were taking her. Then a light bulb went off in her head. "Are you guys taking me to my favorite restaurant?"

With a smile on his face, Aaron looked down at her and said, "What gave it away?"

Ariel clenched her fists in excitement. "Oh, nothing. It was just a guess." They turned the corner, and Ariel said, "Did you guys make a reservation?" Aaron and Eric looked at each other, knowing they'd forgotten to make a reservation. Aaron lied and said yes to Ariel to ease her mind. She bought it, but they knew it wouldn't matter.

They reached the restaurant, and it was pitch black in the building. Not a single light was on in the restaurant. She said, "What? They can't be closed!" Feeling upset, she noticed that Aaron and Eric were completely calm about the situation. She was confused and so walked past them to see if the door was open. The door was open, and she went inside.

As she walked into the restaurant, she couldn't see a thing. Aaron and Eric followed behind her. Starting to get mad, she said, "What's going on here?"

Within a few seconds, the lights turned on, and about a hundred people were standing in front of Ariel. They yelled, "Surprise!"

Ariel was almost frightened by the huge amount of people who surprised her, and she covered her mouth in shock. She clenched her fists with a smile on her face and saw all the decorations. She turned to Aaron and Eric. "You guys planned this all for me?" She was so moved by what they'd done for her.

Eric said, "Happy birthday, Ariel."

The guests were some of Ariel's friends, people she'd gone to school with when she was younger, and some college friends. A bunch of Aaron's and Eric's friends joined the party. It was possibly going to be the best night of her life.

One of Ariel's old friends stuck out of the crowd: Chelsea. After the apartment building had burned down, she'd moved to New York to live with her aunt. They haven't seen each other since. They spotted each other from across the room and rushed into each other's arms.

"What are you doing here, Chelsea?" Ariel rubbed her back, feeling her long, luscious hair. Chelsea had grown it out over the years.

"I wouldn't miss your birthday for the world."

Somewhere in that restaurant was Ariel's soul mate, the man whom she was going to marry. She simply didn't know it yet—or who it was going to be.

After the party, Aaron, Ariel, and Eric walked back to the apartment. Ariel walked between her two brothers. She kept looking up at them and beaming, trying not to laugh.

Finally Aaron said, "What's so funny?" Ariel exploded with laughter. Aaron and Eric looked at each, wondering what she was laughing at.

"Did you know you two are part giraffe?" With a funny look in her eye and a big grin on her face, she felt very talkative all of a sudden. "I mean, seriously. You both look like you're straight out of the zoo! We'd better hurry—the zoo cops might catch you!" She started laughing again. Aaron and Eric thought this was going to be a long night.

The puns continued through the night, but Aaron didn't say anything about it. For years, Aaron and his brother had made fun of how short Ariel was. He thought Ariel should have her moment to let out all the tall jokes.

She said, "You guys are so tall. You guys are Empire State Building tall. I bet you could touch the stars." Then she started jumping through the air, trying to touch the stars.

Aaron said, "Okay, come on, Ariel." He grabbed her arm, trying to guide her in the right direction.

Ariel said, "Don't touch me! I can go where I want to go." She laughed again at her own jokes. She was surprised that Aaron and Eric didn't think they were funny. "Do you guys live in a town for giants or something?"

Aaron and Eric were starting to get tired of all the jokes.

She kept talking to strangers on the streets, saying, "These are my big brothers. They are giants from giant town." Aaron apologized for what Ariel said to random people all the way home.

A few hours later, Aaron carried Ariel up to her bed. Her took off her shoes and draped a quilt over her. He looked at her sleeping peacefully in her bed, and then he shut the light off to let her sleep. Aaron thought that the whole day was legendary. It was all thanks to that day they'd found Ariel's bucket list in the remains of the apartment fire.

While at the party, Ariel had kept returning back to Aaron and Eric, saying how grateful she was. They could've been mean to her on her birthday, like they used to be when they were younger.

On her ninth birthday, Aaron and Eric dropped water balloons from their window onto her party guests. The guests turned back from the building and didn't attend Ariel's birthday party. She ended up having no guests come at all. Their parents found out eventually, but Aaron took most of the credit for that one. He still called it a classic prank.

Ariel being brought into the Smith family was the best thing that had ever happened to her. She was so thankful that they'd welcomed her with open arms. Ariel always said, "Everything happens for a reason."

11

NEVER AGAIN

The next morning, Ariel awoke with a terrible headache. Her vision was blurry, and she couldn't remember anything from the night before. She grabbed her phone from her windowsill and turned it on.

The first thing that came up on her screen was a missed call from Jordan. Ariel was confused why a person named Jordan called her. She was having a total mental block on who this Jordan person could be. Ariel then saw that the caller had left a voicemail. She tapped the screen to listen to it.

"Hi, Ariel. It's Jordan. I just wanted to wish you a happy birthday again. I had a great time with you at the party. I would love to get together sometime or hang out. Talk to you later, bye." As soon as she finished listening, Ariel's memories of last night started to come back to her.

Ariel remembered why Jordan had called her. They'd met each other at her party last night. Jordan played basketball with Aaron and had decided to come to her party. He was six foot one with brown hair and a heart-stopping smile.

Jordan was whom Ariel had danced and partied with the night before. She felt like it was her Prince Charming who had just called her on the phone. Ariel remembered that she really liked him, and she was happy that he'd called her.

When she went downstairs, the boys weren't there. She figured they'd gone out. Every part of her day was trying. She kept reminding herself, *Never again.*

Eventually, Aaron and Eric did what they always did: tease Ariel about how she liked Jordan. She kept assuring them that she didn't want anything serious. Aaron was nervous: if Ariel found someone she liked, he was afraid that he wouldn't get a chance to tell her how he really felt about her.

Aaron was annoying and followed Ariel around the house. Ariel kept saying, "I'm talking to you about this, Aaron." He kept following her around and asking her stupid questions, trying to get important information. Finally, when Aaron wasn't paying attention, she ran upstairs and locked her bedroom door. Like she had done her whole life, she always had an escape plan. Aaron chased her upstairs, but she had already slammed the door shut.

Ariel smiled. Then she realized that Aaron asking her these questions meant he'd never get his nose out of her business. She realized that she did like Jordan, and she was excited to see where this would lead her.

Jordan was an art major, but he was also on the basketball team with Aaron. He was originally from Portland, Maine, and had grown up with his two parents. He didn't have any siblings, which was why he spent so much time with Aaron and Eric. He felt like he had brothers whom he could lean on and trust.

These facts about Jordan were just coming back into Ariel's mind as she looked at his phone number. She'd been on campus for a while, and she wondered why she'd never met Jordan until now.

Before Ariel met Jordan, she had been going through a very tough time. She was going to the school psychiatrist, and she shut everyone out for the first year of college. When Jordan came over to the apartment to hang out with Aaron, Ariel was always upstairs in her room. She avoided every human being, throwing herself into her school projects and papers. Jordan wondered about the sister Aaron always talked about. He simply never got a chance to see her while he visited.

That was why he wanted to come to her party last night. He assumed that if she was Aaron's sister, she would be fun and awesome like him. The night Jordan saw Ariel for the first time, he realized Aaron had left out one thing about her. In Jordan's eyes, she was the most beautiful girl he had ever seen.

Ariel knew if she started taking an interest in Jordan, she couldn't tell Aaron. If Aaron found out if she'd gone out on a date with Jordan, he would go into crazy protective mode for no reason. Eric was fine regarding whom Ariel would hang out with. Ariel wished Aaron would give her some space for once in her life.

Aaron wished that someday Ariel would see that they could be together. He had had feelings for her ever since the day he'd found out she wasn't really his sister. If he did tell her how he really felt, it would ruin their whole friendship, which was kept Aaron up most nights; eventually his mind would shut off around 1:00 a.m.

He almost woke her up in the middle of the night to tell her everything. He wanted to tell her that he loved her so much he wanted to scream her name through the city at the top of his lungs. Also, he was afraid that she didn't feel the same way, which was why he would never tell her how he felt. He avoided having his heart being broken if she didn't feel the same way.

Ariel had grown up with him, and so they know everything about each other. It was how he knew her favorite restaurant and her favorite color. If Aaron had his way, like he did most the time, he would have Ariel—but he couldn't fathom losing her.

She was his one goal in life. He simply had to wait for the right time to achieve it. That was the problem: he wanted something so badly, but he had to hold back.

12

COURTSIDE CHAOS

Two went by, and Ariel had yet to tell Aaron and Eric that she and Jordan were in a relationship. Ariel refused to tell Aaron anything about Jordan, and so he started interrogating Jordan. When Aaron wanted to know information, he would go to the ends of the earth to get it. He was the most stubborn human being in the world.

Even though she'd made her privacy clear, Aaron and Eric would wait up for Ariel when she was out on a date with Jordan. They would act like parents when she walked through the door. They would interrogate Ariel, but she did not give them the satisfaction. She simply ignored them like she had all her life by not answering their stupid, inappropriate questions.

Ariel was coming back from her most recent date with Jordan. Jordan dropped her off, and she was walking back to get inside. She opened the door and peeked around the corner to see whether Aaron and Eric were still awake. They were out of sight, and so she entered the apartment and shut the door behind her.

She took off her shoes and then turned back around to see Aaron and Eric standing in front of her. She was surprised at how such tall people could make almost no sound. They both had their arms crossed with serious looks on their faces. Aaron had a serious look on his face, which didn't happen very often.

"You guys, I'm not going to tell you anything about Jordan until I know it's serious." Ariel tried to make her way past them, but they stood strong in her path. She couldn't move through their arms, which were rock hard strong. Annoyed, she said, "Will you let me past through, please?" Then she went between Aaron's legs like a toddler.

Aaron said, "Come on, Ariel. You've been seeing Jordan for two months now. Tell us something, please."

Ariel thought, *How fast times flies.* It felt like only yesterday that she had met him at her party. She smiled about how she felt about Jordan, and she thought that they finally deserved to know how she felt about him.

She was about to go up to her bedroom but decided to turn back around. "All right. Grab a seat—this might take a while." Aaron and Eric dashed to the living room like it was Christmas morning. Ariel sat down, thinking about where to start. She was honestly about to them on how she felt about Jordan. She really liked him, and she said she hoped that he felt the same way.

As Ariel talked about Jordan, Aaron saw a look in her eye he had never seen before. She smiled through the whole conversation. Aaron remembered that Eric had pointed out to him that he had the same look on his face when he talked about Ariel. When he would talk about how stubborn she was, or when he went back to an old memory, Aaron had a shine in his eye. Ariel had that shine in her eye—but it not about Aaron.

Ariel was surprised at Aaron and Eric's reaction. They weren't inappropriate, and they were understanding and supportive of the relationship. That they approved of her being with Jordan warmed Ariel's heart.

Aaron said he approved, but inside, his heart was slowly breaking. *I have to stop this relationship before it gets too serious,* he thought.

It was December 3, and because it was December, that meant going to a Celtics game. Going every December was a tradition for Ariel, Aaron, and Eric. There was going to be a new addition to the tradition.

Ariel and Jordan had made their relationship official, and so Ariel invited him to accompany the Celtics game. Ariel bought him an extra ticket, but she didn't tell Aaron and Eric. She hoped that they wouldn't mind. Mostly she was worried about Aaron, because he took traditions very seriously, especially when it came to basketball.

As Aaron put it, "It's the one day where we can all let loose and watch a game courtside." With all of them being seniors now, they had been extremely busy. Ariel hoped he didn't take it the wrong way. Ariel wasn't breaking the tradition; she was simply adding a fourth person to the party.

It was an afternoon game. Aaron had been ready to go since he'd woken up at eight o'clock. The game didn't start until one o'clock, but he was willing to leave at eight to get there. They'd settled on leaving at eleven in the morning. It took them only twenty minutes to get to the Garden. If it was any farther away, Aaron probably would have had separation anxiety.

Aaron ran down the stairs saying, "Ariel, Eric, let's go!" He had his Larry Bird jersey on with his dark jeans and green sneakers. Then the doorbell rang, and Aaron was confused. He wasn't expecting anyone today.

As Aaron opened the door, Jordan said, "Hey, Aaron!" Jordan came in the house full of energy and happiness.

Aaron was confused. "What are you doing here, Jordan? Ariel, Eric, and I are going to the Celtics game. And we should already be there by now!"

Jordan had on a Celtic's T-shirt and hat. "Yeah, it's going to be a good game against the Knicks."

Aaron had a light bulb go off over his head. With a weird face, he yelled upstairs, "Ariel, did you invite Jordan to come with us to the Celtic's game?"

Ariel heard Aaron scream up the stairs. Her heart beat fast, and she started to sweat. She had to come up with something to say. "Aaron, don't be mad at me, but I invited Jordan to come with us. If you don't want him to come with us, I'll cancel. I know how much this means to you." Ariel didn't know that Jordan was already at the bottom of the stairs, and she started to walk down them. Jordan heard what she said. She saw Jordan standing next to Aaron, and her heart sank. She said, "Oh, crap." She pretended to run back upstairs and hide while they laughed at her humiliation. Finally, she came out of hiding and came back down.

"No, it's fine, Ariel. Just promise me he's the fourth wheel. Can we just make that clear?" Aaron said.

Ariel hugged Jordan, and he gave her a kiss on her forehead. Then Jordan said, "Don't worry, man. You won't even know I'm here."

How Aaron wished he had a magic wand to make Jordan disappear.

She wished that her brothers would let her and Jordan go to the game alone, but that was not even possible. One, they would never miss a game when the tickets were free. Two, they probably wanted to keep an eye on her and Jordan. *Aaron more than Eric. Eric probably couldn't care less.*

Jordan said, "You look beautiful."

Ariel looked up at him and said, "Thanks, babe."

Aaron decided to ruin the moment and said, "All right, let's go. We have a game to catch." Ariel grabbed her coat, and the four of them left for the game.

The apartment was only twenty minutes from the Garden, and so they decided to walk. It wasn't snowing for once, and they wanted to enjoy this warm day. It wasn't summer warm, but it was Boston warm, so it was almost fifty degrees when she sun was peeking out from behind the clouds.

Aaron was being a jerk, walking in between Ariel and Jordan. He acted like he was just going out with his buddies and pretending that Ariel wasn't there. Ariel realized what he was doing, and it wasn't going to work. She made eye contact with Jordan to try to tell him something.

Jordan looked down at Ariel and got the message. He realized that Aaron was trying to keep Ariel from spending time with him. Jordan reached around Aaron's back and grabbed her hand. They started to walk slowly while Aaron and Eric walked in front of them.

Aaron and Eric didn't even realize that they'd fallen behind them, and Ariel had a chance to be with Jordan. With every step, they were finally far enough away that they could talk, and Aaron and Eric couldn't hear them.

Ariel took a breath of relief once Aaron and Eric were far enough away from them. It was nice to not have Aaron breathing down her neck.

"I'm so sorry about them coming along. We have this tradition where we ..."

Jordan cut in and said, "Shh, don't worry about it." He stared into her eyes for the first time that day. "I'm just glad I get to spend time you today."

Ariel was touched by what Jordan said to her. Then he walked closer to her and put his arm around her shoulder. They walked together for a while, hoping Aaron wouldn't turn around and notice they were gone. Ariel could still see them walking about fifty feet in front of them, not realizing they were far behind.

Aaron and Eric were talking, and then Aaron asked Jordan and question. Aaron wondered why Jordan didn't answer, and so he turned his head. He saw Ariel and Jordan behind them, walking together. They were laughing and having a good time. Aaron became jealous in an instant.

Ariel was enjoying herself until she spotted Aaron watching them. Eric then turned around and saw what Aaron was looking at. When Ariel and Jordan caught up with them, Jordan said, "Oh, no. We got caught." They laughed it off and continued walking to the Garden.

When they entered the Garden, it was an hour until tip off. Aaron went all out by buying courtside tickets. Normally, they would get balcony tickets, but this time they were going to sit a lot closer than usual.

Once they found their seats, Ariel and Jordan went to buy some food for the game. When they walked far enough away, Aaron said, "Okay, Eric, here's the deal."

Eric rolled his eyes and said, "Why is there always a deal with you?"

"When they come back, move one seat over."

Eric was scared because this was probably another one of his evil plans. "Wait, why?"

Aaron was surprised why Eric wasn't going along with his plan. Eric had never doubted one of his plans before. "So there's a seat in between both of us. So Ariel and Jordan can't sit next to each other."

Eric was surprised at Aaron's scheme. "Aaron, why do you have to continue to try to keep Ariel and Jordan apart from each other?" They were discussing this while the players warmed up. Some of the players were so tall that they made Aaron and Eric feel short. The sound of bouncing basketballs and squeaky sneakers surrounded them.

"I don't want them to get too attached to each other. I'm only trying to shield Ariel from getting her heart broken." Aaron was very quick to tell that lie, because that wasn't the case. Secretly, he wanted to sit next to Ariel. He simply couldn't help himself. He wanted to tear Ariel and Jordan apart so he could have Ariel all to himself. This was the first step to his plan. *Hopefully it will work,* he thought.

Ariel could tell something was up when she walked back to

her seat. She was holding a soft drink, and Jordan had nachos. Eric looked behind him and saw that Ariel and Jordan were approaching. He said, "Aaron, Ariel's heart has been filled will joy and happiness ever since she met Jordan. Please don't try to break this up just because you're in love with her." Eric moved back to his original seat next to Aaron.

Aaron said, "What are you doing, Eric?"

Eric looked at his brother and said, "Stopping you from messing this up for Ariel. Just let her live her life."

While Ariel got closer to Aaron and Eric, she could tell that they were talking about something important. She hoped that Aaron wouldn't ruin this night for her and Jordan. She felt that there was a plot afoot, and she was worried about it. Eric was always the angel, and Aaron was always the devil child. She knew Eric would stop him and try to do the right thing, but she feared that the plan was already set in motion.

Jordan was generous enough to buy Ariel some nachos, which were her favorite. Ariel helped him out by paying for his ticket, and so he thought buying her food was enough to say thanks.

Do you know the saying "Think before you say something"? Well, that was exactly what Aaron should've done before he said his next sentence. "Oh, Jordan, you didn't need to pay for Ariel's food. It's not like you two are on a date or anything."

Eric face-palmed and rubbed his eyes. Aaron had clearly crossed the line.

Aaron could see the fire in Ariel's eyes when he said that. Then he looked away and tried to focus on the game, which was close to starting.

Ariel looked at Aaron in disgust. Eric didn't even want to look at Ariel, because she knew what her facial expression would be. He knew how furious she was. *Poor Jordan. He is afraid to even look up. Aaron and Jordan have slowly started drifting apart ever since he started dating Ariel.*

Her eyes filled with fury, Ariel couldn't believe what Aaron had just said. She took some deep breaths and let it go. She wanted to blow up like a bomb, but she wanted to enjoy the game today, especially with Jordan. She also didn't want to give Aaron the satisfaction of getting upset.

Once the game started, everyone's tension slowly went away. Aaron thought he hadn't said anything wrong in his mind. Ariel was going to unleash the beast inside her when they got home.

During the game, it seemed that Aaron had bionic ears, because every time Jordan tried talking to Ariel, Aaron would join in on the conversation. Ariel couldn't enjoy the game and was starting to reach her boiling point. She couldn't believe how stubborn Aaron was being. It was ironic because Aaron was usually the one calling her stubborn. She'd thought that Aaron was okay with her dating Jordan, but apparently that not true. She'd thought that he was happy and excited for her, but it seemed he wanted to break them up, and Ariel wasn't going to let it happen.

At halftime, Ariel wanted to have a conversation with Aaron and find out why he was being so rude. She got up from her seat and said to Jordan, "I'll be right back, babe." Then she kissed him on the lips, as if she was saying she didn't care what Aaron thought.

With a wide smile, Eric thought, *Ariel has the guts to do that in front of Aaron after all the comments he has said today.*

She then said, "Aaron, can I talk to you alone for a minute, please?"

Aaron simply didn't want to because he knew that she wanted to talk to him about his childish behavior. "But the cheerleaders are about to come out."

Ariel didn't care. She stomped her foot and said, "Now!" Given the tone in her voice, Aaron followed her away from the court.

When Ariel felt they were far enough from Jordan, she turned to Aaron to unleash what was bothering her. Even though the arena was full of people, Ariel was afraid that Jordan might hear her scream at Aaron. "Are you kidding me right now? You're ruining the whole day! Not to mention you've ruined my date with Jordan!" Ariel had never yelled at Aaron like that before. She'd yelled at him before, but never with a beastly tone.

Aaron said, "No you've ruined the whole day by bringing Jordan here! You ruined our tradition—the tradition that started with Mom and Dad."

Ariel was surprised that Aaron had brought up that subject. "What, are you serious right now? You were fine with me bringing Jordan along—or at least, I thought you were two hours ago. Why the sudden mood change, Aaron? Why are you being so vile to me and Jordan? It's not fair to me, and it's certainly not fair to Jordan. You don't even let us have a conversation together. You don't even let us walk together!"

Aaron was upset that he was making Ariel angry. He said, "I'm only trying to protect you, Ariel. That's all."

She thought that Aaron still saw her as a sixteen-year-old girl. Ariel was a woman now, and she was ready to take care of herself. "You can't control my life, Aaron! I'm not your little sister anymore. Oh, wait—we're not even related!"

Ariel tried to walk away, but Aaron stopped her by grabbing her arm. He said, "Do you really want Jordan to break your heart? Is that what you really want?"

Ariel couldn't believe what she was hearing, and she wanted to leave immediately. She broke free of Aaron and walked quickly back to her seat. Aaron followed her, saying, "Come on, Ariel!"

She turned back around with tears in her eyes. She said, "No, don't talk to me anymore! Jordan would never hurt me—unlike some people!"

She got back to her seat, grabbed her wallet, and said, "Come on, Jordan. Let's go."

He said, "Wait, why?" He stood up from his seat to see Aaron rushing down the aisle to get to Ariel and apologize for something.

Ariel said, "Do you want to get out of here?"

Jordan was confused as to why she was so upset all of a sudden, but then he saw Aaron and put the pieces together.

Aaron tapped her on the shoulder and said, "Come on, Ariel. I didn't do anything wrong."

Ariel turned around and said, "You know exactly what you did."

Ariel and Jordan exited the stadium, leaving Aaron and Eric courtside. Aaron saw that Eric was still sitting in his seat after what he'd just witnessed. He said, "Eric, come on!"

Eric said, "But I'm watching the cheerleaders." There was a lot of pelvic movement in the cheerleaders' dancing, and he was enjoying the halftime show.

Aaron said with rage," Come on!"

Eric grabbed his coat and then ran to catch up with Aaron. As he ran to catch up with his brother, he brushed off nacho crumbs that were on his shirt.

Loud music and screaming fans were everywhere while Aaron tried to catch up to Ariel. He tried not to lose her in the crowd. He looked back and saw the players were coming back onto the court to shoot around, but he decided to leave and fix the situation he'd created.

13

BURN

Ariel and Jordan got back to the apartment first so that they could have time to talk. Ariel told Jordan how she felt about living under the same roof with Aaron and Eric. She thought that they still treated her like a child. This was especially true of Aaron; Eric actually trusted Ariel to make her own choices.

She started to cry, and Jordan held her in his arms on the couch. He knew about everything that had happened in her past, and he couldn't help but feel sorry for her. Jordan didn't know what to say to her at the moment. He simply held her tightly and wouldn't let go until she did.

While they were on the couch, Aaron burst through the door with arrogance. He said, "You had to ruin the tradition, Ariel! The three of us couldn't just go to a game like the old days! Now, Eric and I missed the rest of the game to rush home to see if you made it home safe!"

Ariel lifted her head from Jordan's shoulder, wiped her tears, and said, "If you had a girlfriend, you would've done the same thing, Aaron! You would've wanted to bring her along."

Aaron fired back, "No, Ariel, I wouldn't have, because I look forward to when the three of us can just hang out. If you didn't notice, it's becoming less and less, especially because you're spending all your time with Jordan!"

Ariel said, "Oh, wait, never mind. You wouldn't bring your girlfriend to the game because you've never had one!"

Aaron felt that insult go right to his heart. The reason he had never had a girlfriend was because he was saving himself for Ariel. His heart became sore and swollen at Ariel's choice of words. He couldn't see himself with someone else; it wouldn't feel natural.

Aaron and Ariel kept firing back at each other until she couldn't take it anymore. She said, "Jordan, can I stay at your place tonight?"

He said, "Yeah, sure."

Ariel felt relieved to be able to get away from Aaron for a little while. "Thanks. I'll go pack a bag."

Aaron still couldn't believe how the day had turned out. He said, "Ariel, you don't have to do this."

Ariel ran upstairs to pack an overnight bag and stay at Jordan's place for a while. Then it was Jordan, Aaron, and Eric alone in the living room. It was silent until Jordan said, "Dude, I thought you were okay with me dating Ariel."

Aaron looked at Jordan, thinking that he was the reason this had happened. "Well, I'm clearly not okay!"

Eric avoided the conflict, and he slowly snuck upstairs, trying not to engage in the argument.

Jordan said, "I really care for Ariel now, and you can't always protect her. Why do you care? You're not even her real brother. She can take care of herself, and she doesn't need you breathing down her neck every five minutes."

Aaron felt like a fire was burning inside of him. He said, "You know nothing about her, Jordan. I do, and she's been through unthinkable events. She doesn't need any more heartbreak from anyone or anything." He said that so quickly that spittle came out of his mouth.

"Well, I'm truly hurt that you think that I would ever hurt Ariel. That's the last thing that I want to do. Maybe you should think about what's best for Ariel instead of what's best for you for once."

They heard Ariel's footsteps coming down the stairs. She said, "Come on, Jordan. Let's go." She grabbed his arm and headed to the door.

Aaron felt guilty for what he had caused. He said, "Ariel, please don't leave."

She looked at him and said, "No, I have to!" Then she slammed the door behind her with Jordan by her side. Tears rolled down Aaron's cheek while he watched them walk down the slippery driveway.

In complete shock, he felt like he was having a nightmare. He looked out the window to see where they were headed. It started to snow out, and it was just starting to get dark. They turned right, and Aaron assumed they were heading to the bus stop, considering that Jordan had walked here from his place.

Ariel had a backpack on, and she held Jordan's hand as they walked to the bus stop. She didn't turn back because she knew Aaron was out of line. She couldn't take him being right by her side every moment of every day. She felt smothered, and she had to break away.

Aaron screamed in frustration and anger, banging his fists into the wall. He let out a scream as if he was hurt.

Eric rushed downstairs and said, "Are you okay? Did Ariel and Jordan leave?"

Aaron buried his face in his hands, kneeled on the floor, and said, "Do I look like I'm okay? Ariel would rather live with then Jordan then with us, and I don't know if she'll ever come back."

Eric said, "Well, she didn't take much of her stuff with her so, she'll have to come back eventually." Eric felt bad because he knew why Aaron had done what he'd done, and he wanted to help him. "Remember when we were ten and did something to Ariel, and she would give us the silent treatment?" Aaron nodded, still crying into his palms. "She had to talk to us eventually, right? Don't worry. She'll come around."

Aaron's spirit was lifted by his brother. He realized that this thing with Ariel would blow over in time.

When Ariel got to Jordan's apartment, she felt right at home. He lived in an apartment on the other side of campus with four other guys, but luckily none of them were home at the moment.

Jordan showed her his room, and she put her backpack on his floor. She said, "Jordan, I think it's about time I tell you everything about my past. I've wanted to tell you for so long, but now I think I can tell you."

Before Ariel could say more, Jordan said, "Sure, we can talk, but I already know everything."

Ariel was shocked at what he said, thinking he could be a secret spy or an agent.

He grabbed her hands, held them in his, stared into her eyes, and said, "Long before I met you, Aaron told me everything. I was curious about you, and so Aaron told me how you came into their lives. It was a time in your life when you were going to counseling, and Aaron was really worried about you."

Ariel remembered how sweet Aaron could be at times. When he'd made her breakfast for her twenty-first birthday. He'd even learned how to do a French braid so he could teach her when she was six. Ariel wasn't good at braids and that kind of stuff, and so Aaron taught her. But she still couldn't forgive him for what he'd done today.

She and Jordan talked for hours about their pasts together. She clarified everything that Aaron had told him. When Ariel told him her story, it made him feel something more from Ariel.

Ariel did most of the talking while Jordan listened. He lay on his bed while she sat next to him, playing with her long hair and talking about how idiotic Aaron and Eric had been when they were younger.

He ran his fingers through her long hair and felt how silky and soft it was. He chuckled about all the hilarious stories Ariel told him.

Jordan couldn't believe all the stuff Ariel had been through. Given all that she had been through, Jordan was surprised how smart and beautiful she was. He could listen to her talk all night, and listening to her voice gave him comfort.

Luckily, Ariel had Aaron and Eric to get her through these tough times. Given the mental state that she'd been in a while ago, if it wasn't for them, she probably wouldn't be here. They'd helped her pull through.

Ariel rested her head on Jordan's shoulder while she told him stories about when she was young. She shared her favorite memory about her adoptive parents with Jordan. They would watch the Boston Marathon together. Her dad would always claim he would train for the marathon every year, but he never got the chance.

Eventually, Ariel's little heart gave out. Jordan was a gentleman, and he took off her shoes and pulled the blanket over her. Then he swapped his shoulder out for a pillow, which he put under her head. Jordan decided that Ariel deserved to have the whole bed to herself. He decided to sleep in one of his roommates' beds. Dylan was going to be gone for a few days anyway, and so Jordan thought he wouldn't mind it if he borrowed the bed.

Meanwhile, Aaron called Ariel, hoping she would pick up. He wanted to say how sorry he was and that he'd overstepped. He also wanted to tell her how he really felt; he was done putting it off. He was going to tell her this time. He also wanted to make sure she'd made it to Jordan's okay.

Jordan was a good friend to Aaron. They still played together on the school team, but ever since Jordan had started dating Ariel, they'd kept their distance.

Jordan never understood why Aaron acted the way he had. He suspected that Aaron had always been jealous of him. Then when Jordan started dating Ariel, Aaron's jealously went to a whole new level. That was the thing with jealously: it was a deadly disease, and everybody had it. Even though people said they were not jealous of someone, deep down they were.

To keep his mind off Ariel, Aaron threw himself into basketball. Some days he wouldn't even eat. He would always be in the gym working out. Seeing Jordan at practice made Aaron feel worse. On a basketball team, one had to have communication, and when two people on a team didn't communicate, it was the worst thing imaginable. There was a cancer within the team, and Aaron and Jordan had created the cancer.

Basketball came first in everything Aaron did. He thought of a million different scenarios every night before he fell asleep. He would get out of bed and get something to drink. He would think about Ariel and how awful he'd left things. He would stare out the kitchen window until he could feel his body get tired, and then he would go back upstairs to sleep.

14

CAN'T LET GO

The next morning, Ariel woke up from her slumber. She looked at the pillow next to her and realized that the pillowcase wasn't the color of the pillowcase in her bedroom. She forgot for a second that she'd stayed the night at Jordan's. She lifted her head up, looking for him. *He must've gotten up already,* she thought.

She rolled over and grabbed her phone out of her backpack, which was on the floor next to the bed. She turned it on, and the first thing that popped up on her phone was seventeen missed calls from Aaron. She frowned and shook her head. She didn't want to listen to his voice mails.

Then she decided to check her social media. She scrolled through Twitter for a few minutes and then she decided to go downstairs. She grabbed a sweatshirt out of her backpack and proceeded to the stairs.

When she walked downstairs, she realized that someone was cooking in the kitchen. She didn't know who was cooking because Aaron was the only man who had ever cooked for her in her life. Well, except her godfather, David; his denver omelet was spot on.

She couldn't tell who was cooking because his back was turned to her. Then he turned around, and she realized it was Jordan. He was wearing an apron, and it said in big red letters, "Kiss the cook."

He said, "Good morning, beautiful. I made your favorite: scrambled eggs and oatmeal. I also made you some freshly squeezed orange juice." Ariel thought back to when Aaron had made her breakfast, and how he'd made freshly squeezed orange juice. Eric had helped, but she assumed Aaron had done most of the work.

Jordan put all of her food on the table and pulled the chair out for her. Ariel thought he was so sweet for doing this for her. The only other person who was this sweet to Ariel was Aaron. *I am a lucky girl. I have men who know how to cook make me breakfast.* After what had happened yesterday, Ariel really needed this.

"Oh, Jordan, you didn't need to do this all for me."

He looked down at her and said, "Oh, stop that. You deserve this every morning." As she was about to sit down, she gave him a morning kiss.

While she was eating breakfast, she couldn't help but think again about when Aaron had made her breakfast. It had been on her birthday, and they'd had so much fun that day. If Aaron hadn't planned that surprise party, she never would've met Jordan.

While having breakfast, Ariel didn't know that Aaron was calling her again. He was leaving her a voice mail for the hundredth time. "Ariel, please call me back. I'm worried sick about you, and I'm sorry about what I said yesterday. I shouldn't have said all those things. Ariel, I need to tell you something. Something I should've told you since the day I found out we didn't have the same DNA. Please just call me back so I know you're okay." Aaron hung up the phone and put it down on the coffee table. Then he picked up his coffee cup and had a sip.

Eric was just coming down the stairs. He took one look and Aaron and could see the worry on his face. He also noticed the bags underneath his brother's eyes. *Probably because he didn't sleep at all last night,* Eric thought. Eric had heard him weeping in his pillow last night, and he was down the hall. He could still feel the sadness just by looking at Aaron.

"You look like you had a bad night," Eric noted.

Aaron kept staring at the wall, pretending that he wasn't even existing. "She hasn't called me back or answered my texts—nothing."

Eric rolled his eyes, thinking it was Aaron just being Aaron again. *Always worrying and overanalyzing things. These things take time.* He said, "Don't worry. She can take care of herself." Eric didn't know what else to say to his brother to boost his spirit, but he decided to let Aaron try to pull himself out of his slump and stop feeling sorry for himself.

Aaron's heart was swollen from what had unraveled in the last twelve hours. He had awoken to his eyes being puffy and bloodshot from crying and from not sleeping. His phone rang, and Aaron prayed that it was Ariel, but it was his manager. Aaron hit declined and figured this was more important. Ariel was more important to him more than basketball at this point.

"Oh, Eric, she's never going to trust me again."

Eric let out a sigh, tilting his head back while pouring coffee into a coffee cup.

"I don't even know if they made it back to Jordan's place all right. I would go over there and straighten things out, but there's ten feet of snow out there!"

Eric made his way into the living room and sat next to him. "Aaron, why do you think we made her take that self-defense class two years ago? Plus, she has Jordan, and you're not the only one who loves her. Jordan will protect her. Don't worry."

Aaron started to frown. "Wait, Jordan loves her?"

Eric said, "Yes, he does. Isn't it obvious? His face lights up every time she enters the room. You have that same look when you're talking to her."

Aaron wished he could turned back time to when they were younger, so that he would have a chance to tell Ariel the truth.

Aaron felt sick thinking about Ariel and Jordan being together. He wanted Ariel to be happy, but he wanted to be the one to make her happy. He didn't just lose Ariel's trust last night—he lost Jordan's trust too. Considering what had happened last night, they probably weren't going to be friends again unless Aaron apologized—which he hated doing.

"I would give anything to take back what I said. I can't believe this all happened, and it's all my fault." Aaron let a tear roll down his cheek, feeling like the world had come to an end.

Eric put his arm around his brother to comfort him. "Let me try calling her." He took out his phone from his pocket and called Ariel. He put his phone to his ear and within a few seconds heard Ariel's voice. "Ariel, hi. You okay?"

Aaron let out a sigh of relief, and his eyes almost popped out of his head. He was mad because he knew that Ariel was avoiding his calls.

Eric went into the other room to talk to Ariel alone. Ariel knew that Aaron would probably be listening in on the conversation, and so Eric did what he was told.

Aaron threw his hands up in the air because he knew Ariel still didn't want to talk to him. *That's why she's been avoiding all my calls.* Eric went in the other room so that Aaron wouldn't get any more furious than he already was. Aaron turned around, still seeing the holes in the wall when he'd punched the wall.

Aaron needed to cool off, and so he put a coat on and went outside to get some fresh air. For some reason, the feeling of cool winter air always calmed Aaron down. He stood out on the porch with snow up to his knees, trying to have the cold calm him down. He stood outside in the cold to get his blood pressure down. He watched the snow fall off the trees across the street.

Eventually, Eric came outside to join his brother and tell him how Ariel was doing. They stood side by side while the wind blew all around them. Aaron said, "She doing okay?"

Eric looked at his shoes and then looked up. "She's fine. She's going to live with Jordan for a couple of days. Aaron, she said she's not sure whether she wants to come back and live with us. She needs a few days by herself to figure out some stuff."

Aaron let out a laugh and then a cry followed by a tear. "Yeah, she just wants to spend more time with Jordan and not me! I should drive over there right now."

"No, Aaron, don't do that," Eric said. Aaron was about to go back inside, grab a shovel, and dig out his car. Eric grabbed his shoulder and said, "You have to let her go, Aaron!"

Aaron had found out Ariel was not his real sister, he had had a crush on her and vowed he would keep Ariel from falling in love with anyone else. That was why he would try to sabotage and act like a complete jerk when she went out on dates. Every day, Aaron wished that Ariel would be his girlfriend, but Ariel wouldn't let it happen.

Ariel had a suspicion about how Aaron felt about her, but she mostly assumed he was being nice to her. When he would make her breakfast or give her gifts for no reason, she thought he was trying to be sweet after all she'd been through. What Aaron was trying to do was make her fall in love with him. He wanted her to feel the same way about him as he felt about her.

Eric looked into Aaron's eyes, and Eric could see into his soul and how it was breaking. Eric saw that this was eating him up inside. He said once again, "You have to let her go. Aaron, you can't keep trying to make her fall in love with you."

Aaron hugged him, thinking that it was too late. He didn't want to accept it, but he had to find a way. They hugged while snowflakes fell out of the sky yet again, because there was another blizzard coming. Aaron held onto Eric with all his might while tears flew down his cheeks. Due to the temperature and the salty water on his cheeks, they almost froze to his face while he wept. With cold winter air blowing snowflakes all around, the two brothers stood together on the porch. It was inevitable: Ariel was never going with him. Aaron would rather she not exist than be with someone else. *Jordan, of all people,* he thought.

Aaron became a changed man that day. He stopped trying to control Ariel's love life, and he also stopped secretly following them on their dates. He would watch from a distance, and Ariel and Jordan wouldn't even know it. To this day, Aaron never told Ariel that he would spy on her when she would go on dates with Jordan.

15

DREAM WEDDING

It had been four years since the gang had graduated from college. For almost four years, Ariel, Aaron, and Eric had lived in that small apartment on campus. It wasn't until their senior year that Ariel had decided to keep her distance from Aaron.

Ever since Aaron and Ariel had had their big blowout, Ariel hadn't really forgiven him. Sure, they stayed friends, but Ariel had never tried to have a conversation about that big argument. They both treated the fight as if it had never happened.

Ariel didn't want to move back in with Aaron and Eric because she felt that she needed some distance from them. For the last year, she'd lived with Jordan in his apartment. While trying to avoid seeing Aaron, she would come over to the house and get some more of her belongings. She couldn't bear running into him and telling him she was moving. Eric was her secret moving guy.

It would be too painful to see Aaron and talk to him about what had happened between them. They were as close as friends, as family, at one point, and Ariel didn't want to open up those old wounds.

Meanwhile, Ariel and Jordan were very fond of each other. Ariel kept trying to think about when Jordan would pop the question. Ariel couldn't imagine being with anyone else.

It was June 11, and Aaron pulled into a parking spot at a church. He wore a black tuxedo with a white bow tie, and his shoes shined like mirrors. He wanted to look his best because today a very important wedding for him to attend. He owned a sleek black Lamborghini that suited his personality to perfection.

He walked into the church from the back door. The reason he entered through the back door was because he knew that was where all the bridesmaids were going to be. He saw four women doing their hair and makeup and wearing the same colored blue dresses. They were shocked by his appearance and what he was doing here.

Aaron said, "May I speak to the bride, please?" The bridesmaids looked skeptical as to why he wanted to see her. However, one of Ariel's friends trusted him for some reason. This friend stood in the corner of the room with mascara in her hand. She had gorgeous green eyes and long dark hair. She said, "Sure, go down that hall. She's in the second door on your left." She then pointed to where the hallway was.

"Thank you." He smiled when he walked by the bridesmaid who was generous enough to let him pass. Meanwhile, all the rest of the ladies gave him a death stare while he walked past and entered the long hallway.

Aaron proceeded to the hallway. He saw the second door on the left and was hesitant to knock. He then knocked quietly and heard a voice inside say, "Who is it?"

He answered, "It's me, Aaron."

She said, "Come on in."

He opened the door slightly and poked his head through. "Do you mind if I come in?"

Ariel was sitting down in a chair and doing her makeup in front of a vanity. Luckily, she hadn't yet put on her dress. She wore a gray silk robe and white sandals. She turned around and said, "Of course you can come in, silly." She turned around and put her forearm on the chair behind her. They both chuckled in excitement.

He started walking toward her, and the closer he got, the more he realized how beautiful she was. He said, "Wow! You look absolutely stunning, Ariel. Jordan is one lucky man."

She got up from her chair and said, "Thank you, but I'm not even wearing my dress yet."

Aaron shook his head. "You don't need some dress to look pretty. You're already the most beautiful girl in the world."

She tilted her head and smiled at his kind words. Then she looked back down at her feet. "How's Jordan holding up? He's probably nervous, right? He probably wants to go shoot some hoops or something."

Aaron replied, "You know NBA players are arrogant men that play basketball, and they'll always get mad at you went you don't make a call."

They laughed once again. Ariel couldn't stop looking at his pearly white teeth. "Seriously, how is Jordan doing?"

Aaron put his hands in his pockets and said, "Don't worry. He's fine, Ariel. He's probably more worried about playing against me in the finals tomorrow." There was a slight pause, and then he said, "Oh, I have something for you." He pulled a jewelry box out of his breast pocket. He opened it and it revealed something shiny inside. It was a beautiful pearl necklace. Ariel gasped at its shine. Aaron said, "Jordan wanted you to wear this today when you walk down the aisle. His mother wore it at her wedding, and he hoped that you would wear it."

Ariel thought that she should wear it because Jordan's parents had been together for forty years. "Yes, of course. Can you put this on me?" She turned around and Aaron took it out of the box and gently placed around Ariel's neck. Then he clasped the two ends of the necklace together. She looked in the mirror and thought the pearls were the perfect touch.

Aaron said while weeping, "I'm so happy for you, Ariel. I really am." Ariel knew why he was starting to get upset. He said, "Forget it. Today is about you and Jordan. All you need is your dress, girl. Come on, where's the dress?"

Ariel laughed once again at his choice of words. "It's in the closet, but you're not supposed to be here in the first place." She pushed him playfully to get him to leave.

He pretended that her push was very forceful and stepped back a couple steps, smiling. He said, "Okay, fine." Then they both hugged, but this hug was exceptionally long. "This is our last chance to run away together."

Ariel knew that she loved Aaron too, and she said, "Stop it. You're going to ruin my makeup." Ariel started getting teary-eyed while looking at him. Then they awkwardly jumped away from each other at the same time.

Aaron awkwardly left the room with no last words. As he left, Ariel wished things could've gone differently. But she knew the right thing to do today was marry Jordan.

Outside Ariel's room were the bridesmaids, waiting to enter her room. He said, "Sorry, just a quick message to the bride."

One of the bridesmaids said, "Was that message to talk Ariel into to calling off the wedding?"

Aaron said, "No, Sarah, I'm not trying to crash the wedding. Today is about Ariel and Jordan!" Then he walked quickly down the hall to Jordan's room, trying to avoid any more words with the ladies.

Ariel was alone by herself in a big room. She saw her dress hanging on the closet door in a protective garment bag. She couldn't wait to put it on.

Her bridesmaids came through the door. Sarah said, "What were you and Aaron talking about? He wasn't trying to put a stop to the wedding, was he?"

Ariel thought about what would happen if she didn't meet Jordan at the altar, only for him to find out she'd run off with Aaron, his best friend. She said, "No. Stop it, you guys! He just wanted to give me this pearl necklace. It was Jordan's mother's necklace—the necklace she wore on her wedding day."

The girls had smiles on their faces and commented how generous and thoughtful Jordan was. They thought he was a lot more generous the Aaron ever would be. Then the girl with the dark and hair and green eyes said, "Okay, let's put on the dress." She took it off the closet handle.

Ariel said, "Be careful with that dress, Molly. Don't drop it."

Molly said, "Well, then, let's get you into it."

Back at the groomsmen's room, Jordan stood in front of a mirror and put on his suit. When he saw Aaron enter the room, he started asking a million questions a minute. "Is she nervous? Don't tell me she's nervous. Please don't. What kind of dress did she get? Did you give her my mom's necklace?"

Aaron put his hands on Jordan's shoulders and said, "Calm down. Yes, I gave her the necklace, and she's fine. Dude, come on. You're getting married to the best woman in the whole world." Aaron knew that, of course, because that was what he thought of Ariel.

Jordan said, "Yeah, I know. I'm just a little nervous, that's all. I mean, who wouldn't be nervous on their wedding day?"

Eric came into the room and said, "Forty-five minutes, everybody. Jordan, that's only forty-five minutes until you're standing at the altar." Eric's words made Jordan feel more nervous.

Aaron said, "Thanks for the countdown, bro." He gave Eric a look as if Eric hadn't needed to say that. Jordan was already nervous enough.

Truthfully, Jordan was more nervous than excited. He wanted everything to go perfect because that was what Ariel deserved. He hoped that Ariel didn't having any second thoughts about marrying him. Then he started to imagine what she was doing this very moment.

Ariel was getting into her wedding dress. Molly was zipping up the back of her dress. Ariel took in a deep breath and turned around to see herself in the mirror. Before she could turn around, she'd already started crying.

Molly said, "Please tell me those are happy tears. Stop it—you don't want to ruin your makeup."

Ariel grabbed a tissue and wiped a tear off her cheek. "They're happy tears, all right. I can't believe today is the day."

They both laughed with joy. Ariel then turned around to see herself in the mirror. Ariel wore a mermaid dress with a crystal diamond belt around her waist. Her hair was up in a braided bun, with two pieces of hair flowing down both sides of her face. The pearl necklace was just the right amount of jewelry.

She walked out of the changing room and showed herself to the rest of her friends. They gasped at her beauty. Ariel wasn't much of a dressy girl, but she could pull off a wedding dress. She spun around showing the back of the dress. The bottom of the dress flowed with her as she spun. They all thought she looked absolutely stunning.

The bridesmaids left Ariel alone for a few minutes. She wanted to gather her thoughts before she walked down the aisle. She kept looking in the mirror and seeing her beauty on the outside for a change. Most of the time she wouldn't see herself as beautiful or pretty, but today she did. She then said, "I'm ready to get married."

Ariel awoke, kicking around and sweating through her shirt. She had dreamed up the wedding. She heard her chest pounding and her ears ringing. Jordan lay beside her, and he woke up as well. He said, "Hey, you okay?"

Ariel wasn't really sure. She couldn't believe that she'd just dreamt that up. She said, "Jordan, I know we've been together for a few months, but I'm breaking up with you."

Jordan rubbed his eyes and then said, "What? Ariel, what? Are you sure you're not sleep talking?"

Ariel rolled out of bed started to put her clothes on over her pajamas. "I'm sorry, Jordan, but I can't be with you anymore. My heart doesn't lie with you."

"What a minute. Is this about us, and me not making a commitment?" Jordan couldn't believe what he was hearing.

Ariel said, "No, Jordan. I've just loved someone for a lot longer without knowing it, and I'm sorry." No more words were said, and Ariel walked out of Jordan's life.

Ariel ran down the stairs while checking her phone. Aaron had given up calling her months ago. Ariel had been living with Jordan for a while, and hasn't seen or heard from Aaron in quite some time. She went to voice mail on her phone and decided to listen to all of the messages Aaron had left her in the days after their big fight.

She put on her coat and decided to walk back to Aaron and Eric's house. While she walked, she had her phone up to her ear, listening to Aaron's voice. She started crying by the sound of his voice and how sorry he was. In most of his messages, he kept saying that he needed to tell her something, but he had to tell her in person.

Ariel wondered why he'd stopped trying to contact her all of a sudden. She kept thinking if she hadn't had that dream, she would've never seen how Aaron was the one with whom she belonged. Aaron was the one she loved. She had simply never admitted it to herself. She hoped it just wasn't too late to make things right.

It was extremely early in the morning. She could see that the moon was still out from the night before, and the sun was just about ready to come up for the day. Ariel was freezing and wished she'd grabbed one of her warmer coats, but she was already too far away from Jordan's apartment to turn back. Determination drove her to walk as fast as she could toward Aaron's house. She was also trying to not slip on the icy sidewalks. Still she listened to the voice mails Aaron had left her months ago. She had been strong enough to not listen to them until now, but she hadn't deleted them off her phone.

Oh, how she wished to be by a warm, cozy fire right now. She knew that the cold would be over soon, and she could almost see Aaron's house. It wasn't that far from where she was. She stuck her phone back in her pocket while she rapidly walked closer to his house.

16

DECISIONS

Ariel finally reached her old house. As she walked down the driveway, she started thinking about all of the hints Aaron had tried to give her over the years. There were numerous times where Eric had almost blown Aaron's cover.

She remembered when Eric had teased her about someone who had a crush on her. Ariel didn't want to hear about it, but it turned out it was Aaron all along. When he had been a jerk the night of the Celtics game, he had simply been jealous that he couldn't be with her.

A lot of memories went through Ariel's mind as she walked up to the doorstep of her old house. Ariel knew that Aaron was her soul mate. She wished she had never pushed him away.

She banged on the door with her fist and then said, "Aaron, it's me. Open up!" She continued banging until the door was finally open.

It was Eric who opened the door, and he was surprised to see her. She said to him," Oh, Eric." She hugged him and then went inside. Even though Aaron and Eric were identical twins, Ariel could still see the differences in both of their personalities.

"Ariel, what are you doing here?"

She pulled away from him and said, "Where's Aaron? I need to talk to him! Is it true? Does Aaron really love me?"

Still sleepy, Eric was shocked by what Ariel asked him. He figured that he had to give her the news at some point. He simply hadn't thought it would be this early in the morning. "Yes, Ariel he does. He's been in love with you ever since he found out you weren't a Smith."

Ariel took some deep breaths and said, "Why didn't he tell me that? We could've been together!" Her voice became intense and furious as to why Aaron had hidden his love from her all these years. She was more mad at Eric for not telling her anything.

"Ariel, he was afraid that he would ruin your friendship if he told you he had feelings for you. That was the last thing he wanted to do."

With all that in mind, she sat down on the couch. She shook her head and then said, "Where is he? I have to talk to him?" Then she stood back up.

Eric gave her a worried look. "He didn't tell you, did he?"

"Tell me what, Eric?" Now Ariel wished she had listened to his voice mails sooner.

Eric said, "Aaron is in Germany."

Ariel thought, *What the hell could he be doing in Germany?* "Germany?" she said aloud.

"Yeah. He was going to tell you, but he wanted to tell you in person. When you moved in with Jordan, he decided to take the deal."

"Wait a second. What deal?"

Eric was afraid to tell her the rest, but he said, "He took the deal to go play basketball for a German team for four years. When you clearly wanted nothing to do with him, the choice became easier for him. Ariel, he let you go." Eric was afraid because this kind of information could trash her mind and set her back.

She said, "The love of my life is all the way in Germany?"

"Ariel, he didn't want to go, but the only reason for him to stay was you. Once I told him you were moving in with Jordan, he decided to go to Germany."

It felt like a knife plunged through Ariel's heart when Eric said those words. She started to tremble while she closed her eyes. Her hands shook, and she gasped, thinking the unimaginable.

"He didn't want to leave you, Ariel, but he decided to chase his dream. He couldn't chase you anymore. Trust me—it was one of the hardest decisions in his life."

Ariel couldn't believe that Aaron was all the way in Germany—and that she was the one who could've kept him here. "When did he leave to go there?" Ariel faced away from Eric and stared at the wall.

"He's been there for two months."

Ariel didn't know what to do. Her heart was shattered from a lot of things. It was like a wave of emotions had collapsed on her. Her parents being killed and not being able to fine the murderer. Her childhood home burned down to the ground. Her adoptive parents being killed in that fire. However, losing Aaron was the saddest thing she had ever gone through.

Eric said, "What are you going to do?"

She turned around and looked at Eric and said, "I don't know. I need to get away." She pressed her lips together while her eyes filled up with tears. Then she walked out the front door with no further words.

"Wait, Ariel! Where are you going?" She didn't answer him she walked down the driveway. As she was closing the door, she covered her face so he couldn't see her weeping. Eric was going to go after her, but he had no shoes on, and he was in his blue bathrobe. He knew what he had to do: call Aaron. Because Aaron was all the way in Germany, the time zone was different. In Boston, it was early in the morning, and in Germany is was late at night. Eric didn't care what time it was. He knew that Aaron would want to hear this.

Aaron was strolling through the streets of Berlin with a sweet

German girl holding his hand. She spoke English, and Aaron was thankful because he didn't know any German at all. She had a German accent, which he found very attractive.

Ebony was a beautiful woman. She had long dark hair and misty green eyes. She wore a tight black dress that went above her knees with a large fur coat covering her shoulders. Ebony wore black high heels that made her legs appear to go on forever.

They walked back to his apartment after their date. They were laughing and having a good time, and for the first time Aaron felt that he had gotten over Ariel. All of a sudden, his phone rang. He took it out of his pocket and saw Eric's name on his phone.

His date said, "Are you going to answer that?"

Aaron said, "No, it's just my brother."

She was confused as to why he didn't answer it. "What if it's important?"

Aaron thought Ebony was right, because it might be an emergency. "Hello, Eric. What is it?" Ebony looked at him with a smile. Aaron could strangle his brother right now for interrupting his date.

"Aaron, you have to come back. It's Ariel—she loves you. She put all the pieces together. But I told her you were in Germany."

Ebony started kissing Aaron on his neck to get him to hang up the phone. Aaron said, "What? Really?"

"Yes, really. I told you, Aaron. You should've told Ariel you were leaving for Germany before you left."

Aaron started to get distracted by Ebony. "Where is she?"

Eric said, "I don't know. She ran off after she came over to talk to you and apologize."

Aaron couldn't believe that Ariel had come over to apologize. Assuming she'd broken things off with Jordan, that meant she had come back to be with Aaron for real. "Well, have you gone out and looked for her yet?"

Eric was annoyed at his tone. "Well, I was going to but, I wanted to call you first."

Aaron let out a mad sound and said, "Look for her. I'll get on a flight." Then he hung up.

Ebony looked at Aaron, concerned. "Is everything okay, Aaron?"

Aaron put his phone back in his pocket. He took Ebony's hands off his waist and said, "I'm sorry. I can't do this. I'm in love with someone else." Then he sprinted to his car. His hair flowed through the wind, and he didn't look back at Ebony.

Ebony yelled out, "Aaron wait!" He didn't hear her, and she was left standing in the cold saying, "Oh, my god! Oh, my god!"

Aaron got to his car and checked his phone. He called Ariel immediately, hoping she would pick up. She didn't, and he threw his phone on his dash board, frustrated. He pulled out of his parking spot and drove away, making the tires screech. He was headed to the Berlin airport.

While he drove, he picked up his phone again to look at flights from Berlin to Boston. There was a ten o'clock flight, and it was exactly nine o'clock. The airport was ten minutes away; he knew he could make it in time. He simply had to pass all these pokey drivers that drove extremely slow.

He didn't have anything packed to go with him to Boston, but he figured he was enough to surprise Ariel. He had enough money on his credit card for the flight. He forgot one thing, though. If he was to leave Germany, he would be leaving his dream of playing basketball for a professional team. He had to either stay in Germany or go after the girl he'd loved for years. For Aaron, the choice was easy.

Basketball was only a small part of what Aaron had set his eyes on to do in life. After he retired from playing basketball, he had his life all planned out. He'd marry Ariel and start a family. While he thought about that, his throat became dry. His eyes became red and watery, and his stomach was in knots.

He pulled into a parking spot at the airport. He swung his door open, hitting the other car next to him. He didn't even flinch because he didn't care. He ran to go into the airport and ran through the front doors. The first thing he had to do was book a flight to Boston. Luckily, there was one seat left on the flight.

Once he got through security, he had to board the plane. Once he got to the right check-in section, he saw a flight attendant at the desk. He sprinted over to her. He was breathing heavily and could not speak.

The lady said, "May I help you, sir?"

Aaron took some quick breaths and then he said, "Is Flight 101, Berlin to Boston, still boarding?"

The lady said, "Oh, I'm sorry, sir. I'm afraid you've missed it."

Aaron was so mad at himself. If he hadn't been out on a date with Ebony, he probably would've made the flight in time. He said, "Okay, what's the earliest flight I can get to Boston, Massachusetts, tomorrow?"

The lady looked at her computer. "Well, sir, the rest of our flights have been cancelled. Flight 101 was the last plane to take flight because there's big storm coming in tonight, and it's due to continue throughout this weekend. No planes will be able to fly."

"So you're telling me there are no more planes going to Boston from now through the end of this weekend?"

There was a pause, and then she said, "I'm sorry, sir. There will be no further flights to Boston until Monday morning. Hopefully that will be when the storm has stopped."

"But today is Friday. I can't wait until Monday!" Aaron had never been so mad in his life. Well, not having Ariel in the first place was very upsetting, but this was another level. The storm was keeping Aaron from getting on a plane to get back to Boston.

As Aaron walked away the lady said, "Well, there is one plane you could get on."

Before she could say anything else, Aaron said, "What plane, miss? If you're telling me there are no planes until Monday morning, I'm better off swimming back to Boston!" Aaron's eyes were almost popping out of his head, and a vein in his neck was visible. e slammed his hands on the desk and gave her his passport very firmly.

She said, "You want to go to Boston, Mr. Smith?"

Aaron had an evil look in his eye—that look he only gave to people when he needed them to do something. "I'll do anything to get back to Boston!"

The flight attendant told Aaron that her father was flying into Boston tonight. He was delivering supplies from his shipping company, and she wanted to know if Aaron was interested. Aaron would fly back to Boston on a paper airplane if he could get there faster than a regular plane. She told him to go to gate two. That was where his ride back to Boston would be.

At first Aaron was skeptical about this girl's father giving him a lift back to Boston. However, it was either take this flight or wait three more days to get to Ariel. Aaron couldn't wait three more days. He didn't want to wait eight hours, but that was how long it took to get to Boston from Germany.

First, Aaron needed to call his agent. Even though his head was spiraling into madness after getting worked up, he had to tell his agent that he couldn't stay in Germany any longer. He knew that he would be putting his entire basketball career at risk. When it came to Ariel, it was worth it.

He called Damien on his phone right before he was about to leave the airport. Damien was the one who'd gotten him to Germany to try out for the professional team in the first place. Aaron hoped Damien wouldn't be too disappointed on his decision.

"Hello, Damien."

Aaron heard a yawn on the other line. "Aaron, it's eleven o'clock at night. What's wrong?"

Aaron took a deep breath before he said his next sentence. "Look, Damien. I know you've done a lot for me, and I'm really thankful, but there's something bigger back in Boston." Aaron started getting choked up thinking that he was going back to his hometown—and his girl was going to be waiting for him there.

"What are you talking about? If you play pro here for four years, you could possibly be drafted in the NBA. I know that's not a guarantee, but you've got a shot—much like your smooth jump shot. You are my most talented client."

Aaron put his hand on his forehead and covered his mouth. He could be turning down an NBA contract if he didn't stay with the German team for four years. His eleven-year-old self inside said to pick basketball over everything else, but he just couldn't do it.

17

BUMPY RIDE

"I know, Damien. It's just°...." He paused without finishing his sentence.

"Aaron, you still there? Come on, buddy. Talk to me."

Aaron switched the phone into his left hand, and he started to tremble. He scratched the back of his head, wondering whether he was making the right choice. "Damien, I know my dream was to play in the NBA, and I've had that dream since I was a little boy."

Damien was confused as to where he was going with this conversation.

"Well, remember I was talking about finding the one."

"The one being your soul mate?" Damien said.

"Yeah," Aaron smiled. "Well, she's in Boston, and I'm gonna go get her." A tear rolled down his cheek.

"Okay, Aaron. Are you sure? Because once you go back on your word on a contract, it's hard to ever get one ever again."

Aaron banged his feet as he said, "I know that, but I can't let her go. I did it once, and I'm not doing it again." Aaron was not much of a crier, but today he broke down like a baby.

"Well, Aaron, I hope you find what you're looking for in Boston.

I'd still be happy to be your manager if you ever need anything. Do what you gotta do."

"Thanks for understanding."

Damien hung up, probably to go back to sleep.

Aaron looked around the airport, and it was completely empty. Thankfully, no one saw him crying. He wiped his face and headed to gate two. No one was around, and so he looked for the man who was going to fly him to Boston.

He opened the door to the runway, and there was nothing but lights on the side of the building. Everything else was pitch-black. Then a man came up behind him and patted him on the shoulder. "Hey. You must be Aaron." The man was chubby and smelt like cigarettes.

Aaron said, "Are you the pilot who's going to get me to Boston?"

He grabbed a big flashlight and said, "Non-certified pilot Willy at your service. I heard Caroline sent you." Then they walked down the flight of steps together.

"Yes. She said you can get me to Boston in eight hours." Before he could say any more, he was standing in front of a little red plane. It was so small that it didn't look like both of them could fit. "We're riding in that thing?"

Pilot Willy turned around and said, "That thing has a name, and her name is Betsy. Come on. Let's get in the air before the storm starts."

Aaron thought he was crazy to go on that tiny plane. Not to mention he may have a crazy pilot driving it! Willy claimed to sane, but Aaron was skeptical. "Wait—we're flying *into* the storm! What do you think I am, crazy?"

"Here's the deal, cupcake. We're going to fly around the storm. Unlike these big airplanes, which are afraid to fly around a storm. Now, come on."

Willy entered the plane first, and Aaron followed. The plane was only a two-seater. Aaron said, "Are you sure we'll be safe flying around the storm?"

Willy said, "Of course, cupcake. We'll be fine. I've got to get these supplies back to Boston, and I'm sure you've got your reasons to get to Boston as well."

"So, you've done this before?"

The pilot laughed. "Nope!" He laughed again. "Trust me, cupcake. We'll be out of Germany in an hour, and the storm doesn't get real bad until a few hours from now. We'll be far from it once we get up in the air. Then it will be easy, goin' over the Atlantic."

Aaron was willing to put his faith in a man he didn't know. He wasn't even a certified pilot!

"So what is the reason you want to go back to Boston so badly?"

Aaron knew that this was going to be a long plane ride. He figured this old man would want to hear his story eventually. Once they got up in the air, Aaron told Willy why he needed to go back to Boston.

Willy said to Aaron, "Love does weird things to you, but it will be worth it in the end."

Aaron said, "Don't worry, this girl is worth it."

"Yeah, that's what I thought about my ex-wife, Cassandra. She was a beautiful woman, and funny. Oh, boy, was she funny. She could make anybody laugh. One day she came home from the doctor, and it wasn't good news. She had a brain tumor. Little did we know she was ten weeks pregnant at the time, with Caroline."

Aaron knew that was just the start of the story, but he felt that it wasn't going to be a happy one. Just by the tone of Willy's voice, Aaron could tell that his wife was no longer with him.

"Now, Cassandra gave birth to Caroline, and everything was fine. Then one checkup later, the tumor was spreading all around her brain, crushing it from the outside. Even after she had all that treatment, that sucker still managed to kill her." Willy tried to keep his eyes dry.

Aaron said, "I'm so sorry for your loss."

Willy breathed in through his nose and out his mouth and said, "Thank you. Every day I look at Caroline, I can see so much of her mom in her. It makes me feel better to see Caroline every day. I just wish she could've met her mom. Caroline was only a few months old when her mother died. I practically raised her on my own."

Aaron looked at what that man has gone through.

Willy said, "But I got the best thing that has ever happened to me: Caroline. If I had never taken that vacation to Germany, I never would've met Cassandra."

Aaron smiled at the love story of how Willy and Cassandra had met. He looked at his phone, and it said 4:11 a.m. If he was lucky, he was already halfway there. He was very eager to see Ariel and couldn't wait to see her face.

Willy and Aaron spent hours talking about life and their experiences. Finally, Aaron zonked out and fell asleep in his chair. Willy kept his eyes on the sky while Aaron got some shut-eye and rested his exhausted brain. They made their way around the storm perfectly, just like Willy said.

It was five o'clock in the afternoon in Boston. Willy and Aaron were a few minutes from landing the plane. Aaron said, "Well, I couldn't have asked for a better pilot, Willy. Thank you."

Willy said, "Oh, you're welcome, cupcake. I mean, I was on my way to Boston anyway. I'm glad that I could give you a lift. Sorry that I couldn't get ya here sooner, but we've been circling for hours now."

Aaron made a friend on that flight. Technically it wasn't really a flight; it was just two guys flying across the Atlantic. Aaron and Willy finally landed in Boston safely. As they were gliding on the runway, Willy said, "We made it, cupcake."

Aaron said, "Why do you keep calling me cupcake?"

"No reason. I just like cupcakes." Willy smiled because that was what he used to call Cassandra.

It had been almost a whole day since Eric had called Aaron with the news.

Willy parked the plane in a secure area. "Thank you so much," Aaron said.

Willy hopped out of the plane and started unloading his supplies. "You're welcome, kid. Now get out of here!" Aaron knew he had to get back to Ariel, but he wanted to see if Willy needed any help first. The man had just flown him across the Atlantic, and he didn't even know Aaron.

"Are you sure you don't need any help, Willy?"

Willy looked up at Aaron and said, "Don't worry about me, cupcake. You get that girl you've been talking about for the last eight hours. Oh, and did you know you talk in your sleep?"

Aaron had a look on his face as if to say, *People have mentioned it before.* "Thank you again, Willy!" Then Aaron ran off the runway and into the airport.

Aaron entered the airport, and it was complete mayhem. There were hundreds of people walking around and trying to get where they needed to be. Aaron forgot how crowded Boston was. Berlin was like a breath of fresh air compared to little old Boston. It was just a little city that Aaron grew up in; it was his home. His home was in his heart.

He then dodged people to get to the front of the airport, saying sorry to dozens of people. A lot of other people were in a rush too, but Aaron was rushing to get to Ariel. He couldn't wait to see the look on her face when he surprised her.

Finally, he got to the front entrance of the airport. He looked around and saw a taxi not too far from where he was standing. The driver started to drive away. Aaron flagged him down by waving his arms and screaming, "Wait!"

The driver finally stopped upon seeing Aaron wave his arms in his mirrors, and Aaron hopped in. Then he gave the destination to his old apartment on campus. He figured that's where Ariel would be.

He pulled out his phone and called Ariel so that he could hear her voice. Her recording message came through the phone. He wondered why she didn't pick up, and so he left a message. "Hey, Ariel, it's me! I'm guessing you got all of my messages from a while ago. I can't wait to see you and hug you, but I'll be there soon okay. I love you." Then he hung up.

When he said "I love you" for the first time, it felt real. Aaron finally was able to unleash what he'd kept inside of him for so long. He'd had to conceal his feelings toward Ariel, but now he could finally lay it all out in the open.

He waited for a while for Ariel to call back. It was going to be a thirty-minute car ride back to campus from the airport, and it had already been twenty minutes. He was almost back to the apartment. Just to check, he called Eric, but it went to voice mail. "Hey, Eric, it's me. I'm almost at the house. Yes, I left Germany, and I'll be there soon."

He thought it was weird that Eric hadn't picked up his phone. He always picked up. Aaron tried not to panic. The sooner he got to the house, the better.

When Aaron was a mile away from his apartment, he gave the cab driver directions on where to go. "Then just take another left up here, and it will be the last house on the right." As they took that left, he was blinded by the flashing red and blue lights.

He had to squint due to all of police cruisers in front of Eric's apartment. Aaron was stunned at what he saw. There were ten cruisers in front of his house, along with campus police and Boston police. All of the neighbors were out on their lawns, trying to get answers as to why the police were here.

Aaron said, "Oh, my god." He threw two fifties at the taxi driver and hopped out of the taxi. Having just come from a date in Germany, he was a little overdressed for Boston. He wore black skinny jeans with warm winter boots, and he also had an olive green sweater with a black vest and scarf.

He walked into the apartment, which was full of cops. Two were in the kitchen, one was coming down the stairs, and two were talking to Eric. Eric spotted Aaron and immediately rushed over to him. Aaron opened his arms to his brother to hug him. "What the hell is going on here?"

Eric came up from hug and said, "It's Ariel. She's gone!"

"What do you mean, she's gone?"

"After I hung up the phone from talking to you yesterday, I went outside to look for her."

It was hard to understand Eric because he was blubbering while he talked, but Aaron pieced together his words. Aaron's heart dropped into his stomach.

"I looked for her and couldn't find her, so I called the police. I should've gone after her instead of calling you. Now I don't know where she is. Aaron, I'm so sorry. I shouldn't have let her go out there all alone." Eric was hysterical, and one cop took him outside to calm down.

Aaron couldn't believe it. He'd come all the way from Germany to get together with Ariel, and now she was missing!

Aaron looked at the officers, and then he started asking some questions. "When did Eric call you guys?"

The officer on the right said, "The missing woman appeared to have gone missing about twenty-four hours ago. She left on foot wearing boots, gray leggings, and a red sweatshirt. We are doing everything we can to find her. Officer Drush, would you like to ask this young man some questions, or should I?"

"I'll take this one."

For some reason, Aaron found that name awfully familiar. He said, "Drush? Officer Neil Drush?"

He looked at Aaron to see if he recognized him. "Yes, that's me."

Aaron looked down at his shoes then at the officer. "If I'm not mistaken, I believe you used to work under a Detective David Smith at one time."

"Yeah, that's right. He was a very good family man. It was a sad day when he and his wife died in that apartment building fire. Why, did you know him?"

Aaron looked at him as if he would maybe see his father through him. "Yeah, I did know him. He's my father."

"Oh, my god. You and Eric have grown up so much! It's been so many years since the last time I saw you." Drush kept looking at Aaron up and down, noting that he looked like Mr. Smith.

Aaron said, "Well, I don't know if you remember, but the first day my dad became a detective, you and he visited a crime scene together. There was a young couple who was murdered, and my dad found a little girl crying in a closet."

Neil had flashbacks to the day and that crime scene. "Yes, I remember that investigation like it was yesterday. Your dad ended up officially adopting that little baby girl, right? She was his goddaughter."

Aaron said, "Yes, and that's the girl who has gone missing. Her name is Ariel."

18

THE SEARCH

"How long have you guys been searching for her, and where?" Aaron was upset that she'd been missing for a day and no one had found her yet.

"Listen, Aaron. We're doing everything we can to find her. We've got search teams on foot all over campus. She couldn't have gone far."

Aaron rubbed his face, thinking of where she might be. "Neil, it's been a day. She could be in a different town by now! We need to search the whole city."

"I know you want to find this girl as badly as I do, but don't tell me how to do my job."

"I'm trying to help you do your job! You're not doing enough! What if she comes back? She might need medical attention! That's what Eric will do!"

Aaron ran outside to see Eric. Aaron found him talking to one of the officers on the front lawn. Aaron said, "Eric, call me on my cell if she comes back." Eric nodded and decided to let Aaron go look for Ariel.

Before Aaron left the scene, a cop stopped him. "Whoa, kid.

You're not going out there. There's a huge storm coming in. We're calling in all of our search troops."

Aaron thought the man was crazy for stopping the search. "She's out there somewhere, and I'm going to find her."

"No, it's too dangerous. We'll set out new search troops in the morning, when the storm passes. I can't let you go out there by yourself."

Aaron let up trying to get away. He saw search troops coming back from the forest in front of him. He heard one man say there was no sign of the girl. Aaron felt a huge responsibility for this. The reason she'd run away in the first place was because she'd been heartbroken at him moving to Germany.

Aaron thought, *That's why she ran off—because she knew I wouldn't turn down my dream. Ariel is wrong, though. I did come back for her.*

The Red Cross pulled in and started giving warm jackets to the search troops. It was getting really cold, and it was starting to snow. Aaron had an idea, but it was a crazy one. The wind was so strong that it almost made him fall backward. The cop decided to leave him, but that was a mistake.

Aaron saw a bunch of warm jackets on the bumper of the Red Cross van. He didn't want to look suspicious, and so he walked over slowly. After looking side to side to make sure no cops were watching him, he took a jacket and ran toward town, farther into campus.

A cop saw him out of the corner of his eye and said, "Hey, come back here!" He started to chase him, but Aaron was too fast. He ran into the storm while he put on his jacket he'd just stolen. The cop gave up as Aaron ran into the snow and was no longer visible.

Aaron had no idea what he was doing or where he was going. The more he walked, the more worse the storm got. He simply had to start looking for Ariel. No one else would in this storm, and so he had to himself. He didn't know where to start looking.

Almost blinded by the white snow, Aaron couldn't see anything in front of him. The wind was blowing him side to side, but he kept trying to go forward. While calling out her name, Aaron desperately kept looking for her. He looked in alleys and other small places where she could hide on campus.

Not knowing what time it was or how long he has been searching, Aaron was exhausted. His knees started to hurt from walking for miles. He still had no idea where he was or in what direction he was moving. He felt incredibly guilty as to why Ariel had run away.

He looked behind him and saw the same view he had been looking at for a while now. In front of him was a treacherous blizzard with wind blowing the snowfall at an alarming rate. Snow came out of the sky so thick that he couldn't see anything or anyone through it.

Aaron felt like something was burning inside his chest when he thought about when he'd decided to go to Germany and leave Ariel behind. He never would've left if he had known that Ariel had feelings for him. If he'd stayed, he wouldn't be wandering all over Boston and looking for her.

He wanted to be inside with Ariel, possibly curled up by the fire with hot chocolate and cookies with the love of his life. Aaron wanted that to become a part of his reality, but that couldn't happen until he found Ariel.

Tired and weak from fighting the strong winds, Aaron collapsed on a snowbank. He lay on his back and listened to the wind. He figured in the morning, he would be able to look for her some more, and he'd also be able to see in front of him. *Who knows? I could be going all around in circles,* he thought.

With that warm jacket he had on from the Red Cross, he didn't have to worry about freezing to death. He dug himself a little hole inside of a snowbank so he could be protected from the harsh winds. He didn't want to try to make his way back home because then he would get even more lost in the storm. He decided to stay put in that snowbank until morning, or at least until the storm stopped.

It wasn't until morning that the storm passed. Aaron was still sleeping in the snowbank. He stayed there all night, waiting for the storm to clear. His arms were crossed, and his legs were completely covered in snow. He awoke to seeing white; it was so bright from all the snow that had fallen. For a moment he thought he'd died and gone to heaven, but luckily it was just the sun reflecting off the snow.

He sat up, brushed off his legs, and stood up from the snowbank. He shivered while seeing all the snow around him. There were piles of snow at every corner he turned. He then remembered why he was in that snowbank in the first place.

He'd been out looking for Ariel last night, and he couldn't fight the storm anymore. Aaron started looking around at his surroundings to see where he ended up. Nothing looked familiar to him. He thought he wasn't even on campus anymore. Then he looked up. It was a green street sign that said, "Elm Street." Aaron knew exactly where he was. As he looked at the sign, a blue jay landed on the sign. It looked in all different directions and shook off some snow that was on its wings.

Soon after that, the blue jay took flight. Aaron watched the bird disappear into the snow-covered trees. Inches of snow covered every branch so neatly that it looked like it could be on the front of a Christmas card. In that moment, he knew exactly where Ariel was. Aaron started to walk down Elm Street.

He soon saw a familiar house. It was the house where Ariel's parents had been murdered. He remembered the day when he, Eric, and Ariel visited that house. It was like a pinball machine went off in Aaron's head. He knew exactly where Ariel was.

Aaron ran to that house. If there was one place Ariel would be, it would be in there. For a day and a half, Ariel has been missing, and he thought that none of the search teams would have checked this abandoned house. Aaron could feel that Ariel was inside, and he needed to get to her.

Even though Aaron was a professional athlete, he had never gone through an adrenalin rush like this. Not even at the end of a game where they were down by two points.

He trudged through the snow in the front yard, swinging his arms and trying to get through faster. Each step became harder and harder. Then he got onto the porch, he stubbed his toes on the boards as they were ripped off the house the last time Aaron was there, and now were covered with snow and ice. Aaron could not see them so he proceeded cautiously to the door. Then, he tried to open the doors, by grabbing the handles, which were frozen shut from the storm.

Breathing heavily, Aaron had to think of another way to get inside. He looked down and saw that the hole in the door was still there from the last time he was there. Maybe he could fit through.

His head fit through fine, but his shoulders could not fit. Moving back and forth, he kept banging his shoulders, trying to slide them through. His attempt was unsuccessful, and so he had to get in another way.

If Ariel wasn't in the house, then this all would be for nothing. Aaron could walk away without knowing whether or not she was in there. His gut told him that she was in there. *Where else could she have gone?* he thought.

He silently stood there, thinking, until he came up with an idea. With all his force, he kicked the door open. A gust of winter air burst into the entire house.

Curled up on the couch and shivering was Ariel. Her arms were crossed, and her eyes were closed. It wasn't that much warmer in here than it was outside. Thinking the worst, Aaron rushed over to her side. "Ariel!" He put his hand on her neck to see if she had a pulse. He found it and let out a sigh, knowing she wasn't dead. He looked down in relief. He looked at her face: her lips were blue and her face was burned. Aaron thought she had probably gotten stuck in the storm too, and her face had been burned by the massive gusts of wind.

Her hands were wrapped up in her sweatshirt, and he saw just poking up were her fingers. Her fingertips were purple from being so cold.

Aaron put his hand on her shoulder and said, "Ariel, wake up. Please wake up!" He stared at her closed eyelids, waiting for them to open so that he could see her beautiful eyes. Aaron grasped her hands, and they were cold as ice. "Oh, my god, Ariel. Please wake up." Then he started rubbing them, trying to warm them up. He cringed at seeing Ariel like this. He hated himself for letting Ariel do this to herself. It was his fault for leaving her. He couldn't help but feel responsible for how she looked in that moment.

Aaron patted his pockets, not feeling his phone inside. It must've fallen out into a snow bank last night he thought. Then, he returned to grasping Ariel's hands, hoping she would wake up.

At the motion of Aaron rubbing her hands, Ariel felt Aaron's presence. They weren't much warmer then hers after being outside all night, but they were comforting. Ariel's eyes cracked open, and he saw Aaron kind smile of relief.

"Ariel! Oh, thank god!" He kissed her on the forehead.

She was confused to why he was here. He was supposed to be in Germany. She weakly said in a raspy voice, "Aaron, what are you doing here?"

"I couldn't live without you, Ariel. Once you found out the truth, I had to come back." Aaron felt good about saying what he had meant to say over the years.

"What about Germany, though? What about your dream?"

"You're all I could ever ask for. That doesn't matter anymore. I found you," Aaron said. He wrapped his arms around her and pulled her in for a tight hug. He whispered," I love you so much." As he listened for her to say "I love you" back, he let go of her. He turned back to her face, and she passed out into his arms, almost falling off the couch.

"Oh, no!" he said, checking her pulse. It was slower then when he'd checked it before. "Ariel, no, no! You're not leaving me again. Stay with me, baby! Stay with me!" He pulled her off the couch and held her in his arms. "Ariel, can you hear me?" She gave him no response. The reason Ariel passed out was probably the lack of food and water for the past two days, as well as being freezing cold and fighting through the storm to get here.

Ariel needed medical attention, and fast. Aaron took off his coat from the Red Cross and wrapped her in it, leaving him exposed in only his sweater. Then he gave her his scarf and used it to cover her face.

He stood up from the floor with Ariel in his arms. He was going to carry her all the way back to the apartment. Assuming that was where all the police and Red Cross people still were.

He had trouble balancing at first, but then he steadied himself as he walked out of the house. He marched through the snow once again, but this time it was more difficult than the first time. The snow was up past him knees, and he barely made it through without dropping Ariel or tripping.

It was going to be a long journey to get back to the apartment. Aaron had to find the strength to carry her the whole way, or at least until he got her some medical attention. He knew that this was going to be the hardest thing he had to do in his life, but he found the strength and courage to carry her the whole way.

Meanwhile, back at the apartment, Eric was talking to the cops. He was worried because Ariel hadn't been found yet. He said furiously, "You guys aren't doing your job!"

The cop answered, "Mr. Smith, we are doing everything we can to find Ariel."

Eric looked at him in anger and said, "No, you're not! If you were, she would've been found by now! You're not doing your job! If you were doing your job, my brother wouldn't have gone out there last night!" Two officers held him back, one on his right arm and one on his left arm. They pulled him far enough away so that they could calm him down.

The cop on the right said, "Sir, you need to calm down. We're going to find her."

Eric broke away from their hold. "Yeah, well, why they haven't found her yet?" He had fury in his eyes.

The cop on the left said, "Don't worry. We sent out new search parties this morning. We're going to find her and your brother."

Eric finally calmed down and hoped that Ariel would be found that day. Eric hadn't gotten any sleep for the past two days, and it was starting to take its toll.

He looked up at the cop once again with a frown and tears racing down his face. "You don't understand. Ariel and Aaron are all if have left in this world. If you don't find them, there's no point in my even existing anymore."

Aaron wasn't the only one who felt a huge amount of guilt for Ariel running away. If Eric hadn't let Ariel run away, they wouldn't be in this situation. Eric was beside himself, especially because Aaron had gone after her, and now Aaron was nowhere to be found.

19

EAST WING

Eric was stressed out about not knowing where the two most important people in his life were, and he was at his breaking point. He may not admit it, but Aaron was his best friend. They'd grown up together teasing one another, but it was all in good fun. Most of the time they would tease another person instead of teasing each other, and that person was usually Ariel.

Eric sat on the first step of the stairs of the porch of his apartment. Even though there had been a crazy blizzard last night, the clouds were finally starting to clear. In an instant, the clouds shifted, and the sun shined through those clouds. As he could see his breath, and snow and ice was all around him, he could hear plows the next street over. Eric was worried Aaron and Ariel would never be found. The sky turned back to its natural color, which uplifted Eric's spirit. With the clouds moved, the fog that was covering every street in Boston lifted. Eric looked out into the distance and watched the fog disappear into thin air.

Eric saw a shadow in the fog. He wasn't sure what it was, and so he stood up from the step. The shadow looked like a tall man was walking, and he was holding something. Eric squinted, trying to see through the fog.

Aaron emerged from the fog carrying Ariel. Ariel was still wrapped in his coat because he was trying to keep her warm. Aaron was Ariel's hero because no one else would have guessed that she would be in that old house where her parents had been murdered. Aaron figured that Ariel simply wanted to be alone and forgotten, but he wasn't going to let that happen.

With widened eyes, Eric sighed in relief and yelled, "Aaron found her!" Everyone who was on the scene looked at Aaron carrying her, and they rushed to help.

Three medics and a police officer ran over with warm blankets in their arms. Another medic pulled an ambulance around to get closer to them.

"Are you okay, sir?"

Aaron didn't care about himself. "I'm fine, but Ariel isn't—she's unresponsive." The medic took Ariel out of his arms and laid her down on a stretcher that was coming out of the ambulance.

Aaron wanted to stay with her. He followed Ariel until one of the medics stopped him. "Sir, thank you, but we'll take it from here." Aaron was concerned that they were putting an oxygen mask on Ariel.

Soon after that, they started CPR on her. The medic working on her screamed, "She's not breathing! We need to get her to the hospital! Her pulse is dropping significantly." Aaron immediately wanted to go with her. He tried to break through everyone who was trying to help her.

"Aaron, stop. She's going to be fine." Eric pulled him away from the people who were working to keep her alive. Eric looked at his brother and knew that something was wrong. He looked at Aaron's left temple, which had a big bump and was very swollen.

"I need to know if she's okay." Aaron broke away from Eric until a police officer stepped in front of him.

"Kid you need to get checked out. Your head must hurt."

Aaron tried to see Ariel from a distance, but they rolled the stretcher she was on into the ambulance. "No I need to be with her! I need to see if she's okay!"

The officer took a stronger hold on Aaron and looked him in the eyes. "Listen to me! They are doing everything they can for Ariel. You need to get checked out. Come on." It was Officer Neil Drush who stood between Aaron and the ambulance.

Aaron saw in the ambulance window that they were still doing CPR on Ariel. "Why can't I ride with her? I need to know if she's okay!"

Neil yelled over to his partner, "Hey, Dan! Come on. We've got to drive this boy to the hospital. He's hurt bad."

Eric came up behind him and said, "Don't worry, Aaron. I'll ride with Ariel." Eric thought Aaron's mind would be at ease if he road in the ambulance with Ariel. Eric didn't want to lie to his brother, but in this circumstance he had to. If he didn't, Aaron wouldn't agree to go to the hospital. Aaron finally agreed, and the police drove him to the hospital to get checked out.

Several hours later in the west wing of the hospital, Aaron was in room 102, lying in his bed with Eric holding an ice pack to his head. Because Aaron was six five, his feet hung off the bed.

Blurry and seeing shadows, Aaron started to open his eyes. His brother noticed that he was waking up, and so he took the ice pack off his head and sat down next to him. "Aaron, can you hear me?"

With his eyes completely open, Aaron looked around the hospital room. "What happened to me?" he said in a raspy voice.

"You have a mild concussion. Do you remember how you hit your head?"

Aaron thought that he hit his head on a fire hydrant when he lay in that snowbank.

"Aaron, do you remember why you're in the hospital?"

Aaron started having flashbacks in his head— from when he

slept in a snowbank to when he broke through the door of Ariel's parents' house. Then he remembered finding Ariel and carrying her back to the apartment to get help. He tried to sit up and get out of bed.

"Whoa! What do you think you're doing?"

Aaron looked at his brother as if to say it was obvious. "I have to see Ariel."

Eric couldn't let his brother do that. "Aaron, you have a concussion. Lie down." He made him lie back down on his bed and let out a sigh.

While looking up at the ceiling, Aaron said, "Why can't I go?"

"If you do, you'll vomit, and I'm not going to clean it up!" Aaron gave up and lay back down. "Do you remember what happened?"

Aaron tried to think about why he'd ended up in a hospital bed, but he couldn't put his finger on it. He shook his head.

"Well, when you got to the hospital to get checked out, you weren't cooperating. You were arguing with the nurses. You kept yelling and tried to run away from them because you were worried about Ariel, and you wanted to go find her. A nurse gave you a shot to make you sleep for a couple of hours." Scared at how Aaron would take this information, he held his hand to comfort him. "You couldn't control your emotions, and so they had to take care of you."

Aaron remembered a few things, but the rest was a blur from the concussion. He looked underneath the covers and saw that he was wearing a hospital gown. He was embarrassed that the nurses had to give him a shot to make him fall asleep so that they could take care of him.

Considering Aaron had never been much of a fan of hospitals, and that he was worried about Ariel, it was understandable how he'd acted. *I mean, that's probably how anyone else would act if his loved one was in danger.* He rubbed his lips together and felt that they were dry and cracked. "Eric, can you get me some water?"

Eric said, "Sure. I'll be right back." Then Eric exited the room, leaving Aaron by himself.

Even though Aaron had a mild concussion, he was still thinking very clearly. He knew he had to get to Ariel. He waited for a few seconds until Eric was far enough away from his room. Then he jumped out of the bed faster than he would for a Celtics game.

He couldn't see Ariel while he was in a hospital dress, and so he grabbed his real clothes and changed before Eric would come back. Also, he would look like a normal person, and so he wouldn't get caught by nurses.

He proceeded to the hallway and looked left and right to make sure Eric wouldn't spot him. Trying to blend in, he walked like he belonged, trying to not draw attention to himself. There was one problem: he had no idea where Ariel's room was in the hospital. He saw a sign on the wall, and it said, "West Wing." He decided to look for Ariel there.

He peeked into other people's rooms and started to lose hope in finding Ariel's room. The West Wing was a complete circle back to where he'd seen the sign. He thought to himself, *I'm not going to walk around in circles forever.* Then he saw a sign for the east wing and headed there, still trying to keep clear of Eric.

As Aaron walked down the hallway of the east wing, he started to worry. What if Ariel wasn't even in this hospital? It was possible that they'd taken her to a different hospital. Each room was concealed by a hospital curtain so he couldn't see the patient inside. Aaron decided to peek through each curtain to find Ariel.

In the first room, he saw a women who looked nothing like Ariel. She had hair dark as night and caramel-colored skin. Aaron moved on to the next room.

Aaron quickly looked at almost every room of the east wing. He was starting to lose hope in finding her. Yes, Eric had said she was fine, but Aaron wanted to see for himself.

There was one room he had passed, and the curtain was half

closed. He saw beautiful, long, blonde hair from the corner of his eye. Aaron came to a stop and questioned what he had just seen. He turned back around. Aaron knew that hair from anywhere. He could spot it out of a line of blondes. Her hair was cascading down the side of her pillow.

He took a deep breath before he entered the room, scared of what Ariel would think of him and how she would feel about him. He hoped that she would take him back and be his wife.

What if all this was a waste, and Ariel didn't really mean what she'd said to Aaron a few days ago?

He closed his eyes for a moment and then proceeded into her room. Whatever was going to face them, they were going to get through it together no matter what. Aaron remembered she was in bad shape the last time he'd seen her.

20

COMING TRUE

As Aaron turned the corner, he saw the girl he loved tremendously injured. Ariel's face was red and appeared to be burned from the snow blowing back in her face. Her hands were covered in big bandages. *Probably from clawing through the snow at night,* Aaron thought. Her hands were covered in blisters the size of dimes.

He took another step forward and saw that her lips were still blue, but not as blue as they'd been the last time he'd seen her. Being out in the frigid temperatures was the reason for Ariel's lips looking as blue as an ocean.

Feeling a tremendous amount of guilt, Aaron saw her file on the counter next to the sink. He slid the file off the counter and into his hand, and he sat down in the chair that was next to her bed. Concerned about her how this whole situation affected her body, he opened the file to check whether Ariel was going to be okay.

Under the word "Condition," it said in bold letters, "Patient was exposed to the harsh temperatures, and from that action patient caught hypothermia and bronchitis. The patient has severe cuts to palms and wrists on both hands. Also, patient suffered windburn to the face and neck."

Aaron looked up from the folder at Ariel and felt horrible about what he had caused. If he had only told her sooner how he really felt, then she wouldn't be in a hospital bed right now. Actually, that wouldn't have helped either because it would've ruined their friendship.

Aaron's mind went back to a time when he was younger. It was the first time his mother told him and Eric that Ariel wasn't really their true sister. His mom was folding his laundry in their bedroom. Aaron was on his bed and playing on his laptop, and Eric on his bed reading.

"Now, I don't expect you to treat her like family. Please at least treat her like a friend," their mother said. When she told them about Ariel's story, Aaron shut his laptop and sat up straight to hear more. He then looked across the hall to see Ariel's door shut. *Is this really true? I'm not related to Ariel, and she's not really a Smith?*

At first Aaron hated the idea, but he grew to love her. Ever since the day his mother had told him that Ariel wasn't really his sister, he'd wanted to tell her the truth. He couldn't though, because his parents told him that they should be the ones to tell Ariel when the time was right.

Slightly grasping her severely injured hand in his, Aaron wanted Ariel to feel his presence. Getting choked up, he said, "I'm so sorry this happened. I'm so sorry." He tried to not grasp her hand too hard, because of the thick bandages around her palm and fingers. He didn't want to harm her more than he already had. "You're my rock, Ariel, and I'll never walk away from you again." Aaron let his head rest next to her on the bed while weeping into the hospital blanket. He couldn't believe that this had happened. "I'm so sorry. I never meant for any of this to happen."

Then he felt her hand grasp his. "I never thought I'd see the tough Aaron Smith weep." Ariel was awake and completely aware. He looked up from the bed and saw that Ariel's eyes were open and beautiful as ever.

"Oh, my god. Don't do that to me!" He wrapped his arms around her and sat next to her on the bed.

"You came back?" Ariel was surprised that he'd given up his dream he had been talking about ever since he'd been a kid.

Aaron responded, "Of course I came back. I love you." His head rested on top of hers.

Ariel said, "Stop it—we're making a scene!"

Aaron wiped the tears off her face for her, considering that her hands were unable to function. She smiled at his kindness, and he said, "There's that smile I've been waiting to see."

"Do you think we can make this work?" Ariel looked up at him and saw that passion in his eyes.

"Will you go out with me?" he asked.

Laughing together, they thought about going out on their first official date. Ariel said, "Yes, I will go out with you."

Aaron kissed her forehead and let silence fill the room. He forgot for a moment that he was in a hospital. He and Ariel were together, and that was all that mattered to him.

Eric burst through the curtain door with a gust of wind behind him. "There you are, Aaron! I've been looking everywhere for you." Laughing inside, Ariel loved that Aaron was so stubborn when it came to resting or taking time off. *He can't go a day without having something to do.*

"You should be sleeping, Aaron," Eric admonished.

Confused, Aaron looked at his brother. "I can't rest right now."

It's best for him to get some rest, Eric thought. "Why not?"

Aaron looked down at Ariel and back at his brother. "Priorities."

Upon hearing that, Ariel had never felt more special than she did in that moment. She started having flashbacks as to why she'd run away that night. She was brokenhearted from Aaron being all the way across the country, thinking he had moved on.

From that kind of news, she was afraid that it would set her back in her studies. She wouldn't be able to focus. She feared not being able to graduate in the spring from a setback like this.

Her professor said if she doesn't get her grades up by the end of the semester, she would not graduate. Now, realizing that she finally had what she had been waiting for her whole life, she had all the motivation in the world.

Knowing the end of the semester was coming up, she knew that it was going to be hard to get her grades up. She thought it would be easier if she paid Eric to do all of her homework for her, but what was the use of that? She couldn't use him like she had in the seventh grade. Ariel was getting good, solid grades, but it was really all Eric's doing.

After putting the pieces together, Ariel finally figured out why Aaron had been so overprotective of her growing up, spying on her all the time, and trying to sabotage any date she had. He didn't do it because he wanted to be a jerk. He did it because he loved her.

The next day, Ariel was cleared to go home. She moved back into her old apartment with Aaron and Eric. She really missed the old place. Besides having a big fight with Aaron, they had a lot of sweet memories in that apartment. She was surprised that they still hadn't fixed the wall where Aaron had punched it out of frustration.

A lot of times at night, Ariel would be up late studying for an important exam. Aaron would tease her and try to throw her focus off. Luckily, Eric was the one to actually help Ariel and not throw off her concentration.

Aaron would throw off her focus, putting his arms around her and kissing her neck while she typed on her laptop. "Aaron, please. I have to get this done." Like always, Aaron didn't care.

When it was time for Ariel to wake up for class, Eric would be the one to wake her up. As Ariel threw out Eric's alarm clock he gave to her years ago. The reason she threw it out was, because of the annoying alarm noise it made, and trust me it was not pleasant. Ariel and Aaron were sleeping in her room, and Eric would wake both of them up on purpose. For fun, Eric would press his bullhorn, waking them up in an instant. He received dirty looks from Ariel and his brother, but Eric enjoyed every second. "Come on, you two. Time to get up!" When they were growing up Eric, would jump on his bed and scream from the top of lungs just because he wanted to. Still after all the years, Eric is the one to still wake him up every morning. If he didn't, he probably would just stay in bed all day if he didn't have basketball practice.

Annoyed by his brother, Aaron grabbed a pillow out from under his head and threw it at him to try to get him to leave. Eric would dodge his throw every morning, but Ariel would get up, which made Aaron finally get out of bed too.

When their mom would come in and check on them, she would say, "What was that noise?" Eric would always blame his brother for it. She knew it was Eric all along, because she could read him like a book, and Aaron hated getting out of bed in the morning. Aaron would wake up sleepy and tired, but he would see Ariel and then act chipper and alive.

Ariel didn't mind getting up every day, but she knew that Aaron would prefer staying in bed and cuddling with her. She couldn't do that.

Aaron would try to take the bullhorn away from Eric, and Ariel had to go to class. It was crucial to not miss any more classes if she wanted to graduate in the spring.

Giving the last push, Ariel was going to graduate. She got her grades up and made the average mark where she could graduate. Ariel felt a sense of achievement and success.

Ninety-nine dates later, it was the night before graduation day. Aaron planned a romantic candlelight dinner. It was a symbol of all her hard work, and he wanted to be labeled as a romantic. He was not just a good boyfriend, but boyfriend who did sweet gestures.

They sat across from each other, and Ariel said, "This is lovely,

Aaron. I can't believe you did all this." She smiled, and the light of the candles reflected off the shimmer in her eyes.

"Well, you deserve it. And I had a little help."

Eric came around the corner looking like a chef from Italy. He even had on a fake moustache to make him look more Italian. They all knew that Eric could never grow out a real moustache. "I have prepared a tremendous dish for your liking," he said in a horrible Italian accent. He brought to the table homemade lasagna. They could see the steam rising out of the cheese on top. "Oh, and please save room for dessert. I made chocolate chip cheesecake."

Ariel thought there was no way Eric could've made a fresh cheesecake. "Really? You made cheesecake from scratch?" She raised her eyebrows, waiting for Eric to tell the truth.

Still talking in an Italian accent, he said, "Ah, yes, well, I'm more a main course chef. So yes, I bought a cheesecake." Feeling defeated Eric headed back to the kitchen to clean up.

Before devouring their delicious meal, Aaron said, "Ariel, I'm so proud of you. From where you were three months ago to now is amazing. You've come full circle, and I can't even express how wonderful you look tonight."

She blushed at his compliments and looked down at her hands. They had once been very injured, but now they were completely healed with no scarring.

After laughing and enjoying a delicious meal, Aaron had one more trick up his sleeve. It was possibly the greatest trick of all. After they finished their meal, Eric brought out the cheesecake. He set it down in the middle of the table. Before cutting herself a piece, Ariel noticed something rather shiny in the middle of the cheesecake. It was a diamond ring that was filled with beauty. Ariel gasped, covered her mouth, and looked at Aaron. She was totally surprised and had no idea.

Aaron stood up from his chair and grabbed the ring out of the cheesecake. He wiped the chocolate chips off the ring with a napkin.

He tried to be romantic as possible and not blow it. Ariel sat in shock with her hand on her heart, trying not to cry.

Aaron got down on one knee with ring in hand and said, "Ariel, I know we've only officially been together for a short period of time. The truth is I want to spend the rest of my life with you." He paused for a moment, trying not to get emotional. "We've been through so much together, and if I have to endure more, I want you to be by my side and be my partner in crime. I love you so much, Ariel. I don't know what I would do without you, and I promise to love you every day. Will you marry me?"

"Yes." She didn't give it a second thought. There was no one else in the world Ariel would rather be with. Ariel jumped out of her seat and hugged Aaron with all her might. They shared a passionate kiss before he put the ring on her finger. It was a perfect fit, and Ariel wondered how he could have known her ring size without asking her.

"How did you know my ring size?"

Aaron thought about whether he should tell her. "I measured your finger while you were sleeping." He closed his eyes, hoping she wouldn't hit him like when they were kids. She did just the opposite and kissed him again.

She figured that he'd wanted it to be a big surprise, and it was. It was the best surprise anyone had ever given Ariel. This night topped her twenty-first birthday by far, because it was the night that Ariel and Aaron became engaged.

That next summer, Ariel and Aaron got married. They decided to have it at their childhood church. They had gone there all the time with their parents and had a lot of good memories in that church. They both thought it would be a perfect place to get married. It was almost like Aaron's parents would be with him through the ceremony.

Beneath the church was the basement, and that was where everyone was getting ready for this special day. There were two rooms to keep Aaron and Ariel separated. They both believed that it was bad luck to see the bride before the wedding. They both wanted no bad luck between them as they started their new life together.

Eric was on his way to see Ariel to make sure she wasn't having any second thoughts. He was obviously Aaron's best man, and so he had a black tuxedo with a white bow tie. His hair was slicked back with gel.

He knocked on the door of the room where Ariel and all the bridesmaids were. A woman wearing a long teal blue dress on answered the door. It was Chelsea, and she was Ariel's maid of honor.

"Hi, Chelsea. This is from the groom." He handed her a jewelry box.

Chelsea said, "Oh, thank you." She smiled. "How's Aaron holding up?"

He smirked and said, "He's ready to get married and is counting down the minutes."

They laughed, knowing how Aaron hated waiting and how very impatient he was.

"Sounds like him. So, everything all set?" Chelsea asked.

Eric triple-checked in his mind then he said, "Yes, everything is a go. Is our bride ready?"

"We just need a few more minutes. I'll give this to her." Chelsea closed the door and said, "Gift from the groom!" All the other bridesmaids giggled and wondered what Aaron could've sent her. Chelsea was Ariel's best friend, and Ariel had also stayed in touch with a couple of close friends from high school.

Sarah was sitting on the couch with a glass of champagne in hand. Julia was over by the window, finishing putting on her makeup. Carly was spraying hairspray and making sure her hair stayed in place. Molly was helping Ariel into her wedding dress.

"Ariel, Aaron sent you something," Chelsea yelled from across the room.

Ariel said, "Oh, he's so sweet."

Molly came out of the dressing room and said, "All right, Ariel, let's see it." Everyone clapped, waiting for Ariel to come out.

Stepping out in white six inch heels, Ariel turned the corner in her wedding dress. She smiled in confidence, knowing that today was her special day.

The dress looked like it was made for her. It was a mermaid gown with a sparkly bottom. She had a belt around her waist with sequins. At the top was a sweetheart neckline. The dress was tight and voluptuous, but she shimmer of the dress added the perfect amount of elegance. Her hair was half up, and the bottom half of her hair was all curled. She had a veil that went down to the middle of her back.

"It's not too much, is it?" Ariel asked. She didn't want to be one of those brides who was over the top with her dress.

Molly said, "No, not at all." They all gazed at her beauty and were happy for her.

"This is from Aaron." Chelsea handed Ariel the jewelry box and one rose that Eric had given her, saying that it was from Aaron.

Ariel opened the box, and the first thing she saw was a note taped to the top of the lid.

My dearest Ariel,

I can't believe that today is the day where we start our lives together as husband and wife. I can't wait to make so many more memories with you, and to laugh over old memories. I made this for you when I was a senior in high school. I held on to it all this time because I felt that it would be perfect to give this to you on your wedding day. It was the semester where I took that jewelry-making class for extra credit. I'll see you at the altar.

Love,
Aaron

Ariel found a handmade bracelet in that jewelry box. The beads were white as clouds, and there was something engraved on it. Written in silver were to letters next to each other. Those two letters were AA to symbolize there love in that bracelet. Ariel melted when she saw that. She thought she was dreaming, but this time it was reality. This was her life, and it only was going to get better.

All her friends had thought Aaron was a jerk when he'd been in high school, but he was actually a pretty sweet guy. They knew Aaron was going to take care of Ariel. They hoped to find husbands who loved them that much.

Ariel put the bracelet on her right wrist and was moved by how pretty it was. She had never cherished something so much before. She loved it more then all of her other jewelry combine. Aaron had made this out of love, knowing that someday they would get married.

She admired the gorgeous piece of jewelry around her wrist. Then she looked back at Chelsea, who held a single rose in her hand. Ariel gasped, thinking back to her very first official date she'd gone on with Aaron. He had been waiting for her to come downstairs and had been casually well dressed, holding a red rose in his hand. Ariel smelled the rose and thought about that first date. This was the kind of gesture that made her more in love with him.

21

DAY OF DESTINY

The wedding was about to begin, and Ariel took a few minutes to herself. She kept looking at herself in the mirror and couldn't believe that she'd found someone who loved her. For years she'd doubted that she would ever find true love. Meanwhile, Aaron had been there the whole time.

The door swung open, and Chelsea peeked her head through. "Ariel, you ready?" When Chelsea said that, she saw that Ariel was still looking at Aaron's beautiful bracelet.

Ariel took a deep breath and said, "I'm more ready than ever."

The church was decorated to perfection. There were white roses placed on the ends of each pew, and violins filled the room with their sound. Aaron nervously waited at the altar for his bride to walk down the aisle.

The priest walked up to the altar and said, "Aaron, it's okay to be nervous." He looked at Aaron, trying to figure out what was on his mind.

"I'm not nervous, Father. I've just wanted this day to come for a long time. I just can't believe it's finally here."

Father Marcus smiled at his love for Ariel. Then he got behind

Aaron, waiting for the ceremony to begin. "Hey, you're a lucky man, Aaron. I'm so happy for you."

Aaron couldn't believe that Eric had stuck with him all these years. He wouldn't have wanted anyone else as his best man.

The music started to grow louder, and people quieted down. It was a small wedding; not more than fifty people attended. Aaron and Ariel wanted to have a small wedding because with more people came more personalities. Also, they wanted to have a small wedding so that they could pay for their trip to go to Aruba for two weeks. Ariel wanted to go somewhere exotic and beautiful. Aruba seemed to fit the bill. That was what she wanted, and Aaron couldn't say no.

First, all the groomsmen and bridesmaids walked down the aisle in groups of two. The bridesmaids wore the same teal dress, and the men had the same teal tie to match. Finally, the last couple came down the aisle, and then the violins started playing "Here Comes the Bride."

The guests stood up to get a glimpse of the blushing bride. Ariel stepped into the aisle looking stunning as ever. She held a bouquet of red and white roses. Smiling ear to ear, she gently walked down the aisle.

She was not much of a dressy girl, and Aaron couldn't believe how gorgeous she looked. Yeah, she probably had some help from the bridesmaids, but in his eyes, she always looked beautiful. The closer Ariel got to the altar, the more gorgeous she became. Aaron thought there was nothing that could ruin this day.

As Ariel got even closer, he realized that she was wearing the bracelet he'd made for her. In that moment with love in the air, Aaron smiled brighter than ever before. His dimple appeared yet again while looking at his bride to be.

He held out his hand to her and helped her to the altar. "You ready?" he whispered.

"I'm so ready."

Father Marcus started the introduction to the wedding while

Aaron and Ariel were side by side. Aaron's heart felt like it was beating through his chest. He had never felt more pressure, not even in a championship basketball game. Aaron practically blacked out while Marcus spoke because he was so overcome with joy.

Time went by, and Father Marcus said, "I believe you both have prepared your own vows."

Aaron felt like time was a complete blur because he was so nervous. He felt like Ariel had walked down the aisle just a second ago. He said, "Yes, my apologies." He turned to Ariel and saw how beautiful she looked. "Ariel, we both know that we have always had a connection. It was simply up to one of us to make the first move. Every waking day, I thought about you. When you finally agreed to marry me, you have to know how happy you made me. I could go to sleep with a smile on my face every night knowing that you are right beside me, sleeping like an angel.

"I love you more than anything in the whole world. I love how your eyes sparkle, and how you make my day better when I'm feeling down. I love how you are kind to every person you meet. Most of all, I love that you love me, and I know I'm not the best person to get along with at times. I promise to love you for the rest of my life, because I do."

There was a laugh in the church for Aaron's joke. Then Eric gave his brother the ring to put on her finger. His hands shook because he was so nervous. It meant a lot to Ariel because that showed how much he wanted everything to be perfect for this day. He looked into her eyes and then he became calm again.

She held out her left hand, and Aaron slipped the ring on her finger. *This is it,* she thought. Now it was her turn to say her vows.

She turned to Chelsea and gave her the bouquet of roses. She thought that was a tough act to follow. She turned back to Aaron, looking at his smile. He hadn't stopped smiling since the ceremony had started.

"Aaron, I have to admit when I was younger, I never would've imagined marrying someone as perfect as you. I dreamed of finding the perfect man who would love me for me. I believe I've found that special man. You've been by my side through the thick and thin."

Ariel paused because she felt that her throat was getting husky, trying to keep everything together. She tried to not cry and to stay composed. She also spent a huge amount of time on her makeup, and she didn't want to ruin it with watery eyes.

"I know we're not legally married yet, but you are the sweetest husband I could ever ask for, whether it's leaving an 'I love you' note in my purse, or if it's buying me a present just because." She looked down at her wrist and saw the beautiful bracelet Aaron had made her. "Or making me jewelry to give to me. I love you with all my heart, and I always will, because I do." She turned to Chelsea once more, who gave her Aaron's ring. Still with shaky hands, Ariel put his ring on his finger.

They both turned back to Father Marcus, who continued. "If anyone objects to this couple's happiness, speak now or forever hold your peace." A few moments went by with silence in the air.

Then Ariel heard a man's voice say, "Yeah, I object!"

The whole audience gasped at hearing someone would object to this couple's happiness. Heads turned to the back of the church, where the man's voice came from.

Jordan appeared at the entrance of the church, and people stared at him with anger. Ariel turned around and almost died when she heard Jordan's voice say that. Her heart beat in her throat, and she closed her eyes before she turned away from Aaron. She had immediately recognized his voice.

Jordan made his way down the aisle and said, "I'm sorry I have to do this to you, Ariel, but you have to hear this."

"What are you doing, Jordan?" Aaron said as he pulled her in close. "Whatever he says, it's not true, Ariel."

"What are you talking about, Aaron?" Ariel asked. *It was a perfect day, but Jordan had to show up and ruin everything.*

Jordan looked at Ariel with power and strength. "Before, you left me for Aaron. I'm letting you know that you made a huge mistake, Ariel!" Ariel couldn't believe that this was happening. "You see Ariel, while Aaron was in Germany, he was unfaithful to you."

Ariel looked at Aaron and said, "You never told me you were with someone else."

Jordan interrupted before Aaron could say anything, "Her name was Ebony Friedrich, and she was Aaron's suitor for two months."

Ariel looked at Aaron again. "Is this true, Aaron?"

Aaron was completely caught off guard, and he said to Jordan," How do you even know that?"

"I have my sources," Jordan said.

"Okay, yes, it's true," Aaron admitted.

Ariel couldn't believe it.

"Ariel, look. At the time, yes, I was with Ebony. But I don't care about her, and I never did. I love you and want you to be my wife. It was before we were even together." He held her hands and looked into her eyes.

For once, Ariel felt like he was telling the truth, but the news was so fresh to her that she couldn't bear to look into his eyes. She looked everywhere else in the church, but she wouldn't meet his gaze. He had kept something from her.

"Ariel, look at me."

She looked at him and saw in his eyes that he was telling the truth.

Aaron bent down and whispered in her ear. She understood and said, "It's okay." Ariel looked back down at Jordan to see he was still standing there. She took a few steps away from Aaron.

Jordan said, "Ariel, you can be with me. I'm a husband who will love you and cherish you and always be faithful to you. Or you can marry Aaron."

Aaron stood there and took those hints to heart. He was surprised at how Jordan had got in here without an invitation.

"Jordan, I left you for a reason. That reason is standing at the altar right now. I couldn't ask for a better man to marry. I don't care that he kept this from me. I still love him to death! Even though he didn't tell me this, it's okay. Everybody has a past. The past doesn't truly tell the whole story of a person, only a small part of it. This was years ago, and I believe him when he tells me he doesn't care for her anymore. I wouldn't want to spend my future days with anyone other than Aaron. You can't change my mind, Jordan. Aaron makes me happy, and I wouldn't know what to do without him."

Then Ariel held up her wrist to Aaron, showing that she was wearing his bracelet. Aaron sniffled, trying not to cry.

Jordan was mad that his evil plan had not worked. He thought that Aaron's secret would break them up and eventually Ariel would come back to him, but that wasn't the case. Ariel and Aaron's love was too strong to break. Feeling defeated and upset that Ariel was marrying Aaron, Jordan turned away from them. He marched down the aisle and out the church, slamming the doors as he exited.

Ariel turned to Aaron to see that he was upset about what had happened. She walked over to him and said, "Hey, it's okay. I still want to marry you."

Aaron looked at her, surprised at how much Ariel still loved him. "You still love me?"

Ariel thought about when she'd made that choice to leave Jordan and go back to Aaron. "I left Jordan for a reason. There's no other man I'd rather be with."

Then Aaron looked down at the bracelet he'd made her and thought about how much he loved her. Ariel wiped a tear off Aaron's face, and she had stretch to reach it even thought she wore heels. Before he got any more emotional, he said to the priest, "Father, can we continue with the ceremony?"

The priest nodded, knowing that this couple was right for each other after all. "By the power vested, in me I pronounce you husband

and wife. You may kiss the bride." They came in for the kiss, and even though Ariel was in heels, he still had to bend down to kiss her.

Applause filled the church as people stood up. The couple walked back down the aisle hand in hand while white rose petals were thrown at their sides. While they walked together, Aaron looked down at her and saw that rose petals got caught in her hair. He looked forward to continue walking to the back on the church. The hard part was over, and now the real fun began.

The band was on fire, playing beautiful music while the dance floor went crazy. Even Eric partied with all the bridesmaids. Meanwhile, Ariel and Aaron were slow dancing in the middle. She rested her head on his chest, and he had his hands wrapped around her waist.

They were both happy that everyone had a good time. Ariel had something on her mind that she had to ask Aaron. "Aaron, how come you didn't tell me you liked me when we were kids?"

Aaron was surprised Ariel asked that question, but he knew that he'd have to answer it eventually. "I didn't want to scare you away. I was worried it could end our friendship. Mom and Dad wanted us all to be great friends, and I didn't want to jeopardize that."

She reached up and kissed him. "Don't you think they'd be happy that we're more than friends? They would be so happy for us. They're probably watching over us right now."

Aaron smiled, thinking about how his parents would react to him marrying the girl whom they took in as one of their own. Then he grew sad that they weren't here to see it all.

She saw that his personality changed in an instant while talking about his parents. Ariel hugged him, trying to have him forget about his past and look toward the future. She too wished that her parents could see them get married. She knew that even though she didn't get a chance to meet her real parents, she felt that they were watching over her on her wedding day.

The music changed to disco music and everyone started to cheer all around them. "Come on this is supposed to be a happy night," she said.

Aaron looked down at his wife and thought about what he'd said today at the altar during his vows. Ariel always made him feel better. "Yeah, you're right."

The happily married couple joined the rest of the group to have some fun. Something caught Ariel's eye. Standing over by the corner was a man Ariel used to have feelings for. He'd almost tried to blow up the wedding, and so she was surprised at his return. He was dressed up for the occasion still. Yes, he'd left the ceremony early, but he couldn't stay away. Jordan stood in the corner, having a drink and still receiving dirty looks from all the guests.

Ariel and Jordan's eyes locked, and she knew that she had to go over and tell him to leave again. She excused herself from dancing with her friends and made her way over to him. She was afraid of what else Jordan had to say, but she wanted to put on a brave face and show no doubt because Jordan was the one with whom she was going to spend the rest of her life. Jordan certainly wasn't going to be the one to change her mind.

Jordan nodded his head and said, "Ariel, I'm only here to say one more thing. I'll always cherish what we had." Then he handed her a wedding present he had hidden behind his back. Jordan started to get flustered, and Ariel could see it. Before she could say anything in response, Jordan continued. "I wish you two the best." Then he got out of there before causing a scene. Ariel let him go, knowing that it took a lot of strength to even come back here today. She thought after his hurtful words, and she knew she would never see him again. He'd even bought a gift because he probably felt bad after making a scene. Jordan had finally let her go.

When she turned around, Aaron was behind her. "Hello, my beautiful wife. Oh, my god—I love calling you that." They hugged with the present in between them. "Oh, another gift. Who is it from?"

Ariel took a breath before answering, "You just missed Jordan, and he wished us the best."

Aaron squinted, wondering if Jordan had really meant that. Aaron and Jordan had been friends not that long ago. Aaron missed him and thought about how they hadn't seen each other for a while. "Too bad. I would've liked to say my peace with him."

Ariel knew what that meant. "Yeah, you would've bashed his face in with your fist."

The after-party was fun, and now it was time to go to Aruba. Ariel was excited to get her ginormous dress off and be able to walk without bumping into someone.

All of the guests were going to wave goodbye to Ariel and Aaron when they drove away. There was a long line of people waiting to see the happy couple drive together. Ariel and Aaron walked hand in hand through the line of people, saying their goodbyes for two weeks. *Two weeks in Aruba is like a dream,* Ariel thought. *And with Aaron, it will be magical.*

As they walked through, the crowded people went with tradition by throwing rice in the air. Ariel prayed that she wouldn't get a grain of rice stuck in her ear, and so she wore her hair down to protect her ears. Besides, Aaron told her that she looked prettier with her hair down. He followed that with, "No matter what, you always look gorgeous, my wife."

Before they got in the car, Ariel was about to throw the bouquet. The bridesmaids were ready to catch it. She threw it, and it landed into the hands of Chelsea. Ariel ran back and gave her one last hug before leaving.

Aaron put the luggage in the trunk and looked back at his bride. He wished Eric had invented jetpacks because it would be a lot quicker to get to Aruba.

Aaron opened the car door for Ariel, and she waved goodbye to the crowd. The crowd of family and friends cheered as they Aaron got in. The newlyweds looked at each other and smiled and laughed.

They could relax now and not be bothered. It was going to be just the two of them for two weeks.

As Aaron started the car, he said, "Aruba, here we come!" Then the crowd watched them as they drove off, starting their new life together.

They had never been out of the United States before, so it was going to be an incredible experience they would remember for the rest of their lives.

When they pulled into the airport, Aaron couldn't help but think about Willy and how he'd helped him get back to Ariel. If it wasn't for him, Aaron would've never gotten back to Boston that quickly. *I wonder what he's doing now?* he thought. He looked at his wife, who was running her fingers through her long blonde hair. He went back to the day he'd found her on Elm Street in terrible condition. She had made a full circle.

Ariel sensed that he was looking at her and she said, "What are you looking at?"

He smiled and replied, "Nothing. Just so glad you're my wife." She reached across the car to kiss him. "Are you ready?"

"Yeah." They both got out of the car, and he got the luggage out of the trunk. Aaron was glad that the flight was only going to be four hours and forty-five minutes. Unlike his flight from Berlin to Boston, this trip was going to be much more enjoyable.

22

A FIXER-UPPER

Two weeks went by, and Aaron and Ariel were driving back home from the airport. They were both extremely tanned from the tropical temperatures and hot sun. July in Boston was a cooldown from Aruba.

Honeymooning in Aruba was the most perfect spot. Staying at a five-star hotel was a treat in itself. They got a couples massage, golfed, and swam with dolphins. At night, they took long walks on the beach and watched the sun go down. Any other day would not compare to those two weeks Ariel and Aaron spent together.

Aaron drove while Ariel looked at pictures she'd taken on her phone. She said, "I wish we didn't have to leave."

He understood how much of a paradise Aruba was and said, "I know, baby. Maybe we can go again sometime. Once we pay off our student loans and buy a house."

"Yeah, I know." Ariel felt defeated because they probably weren't going to go back to Aruba for a long time. They had to go back to their normal lives, and they couldn't pretend to live in a fairytale. Ariel remembered being woken up by the sunrise and going to sleep every evening, watching the sun go down.

As Aaron drove, he went past the exit on the highway they always took. Ariel noticed and said, "Honey, we just missed our exit." Aaron had a devilish look on his face, like when he had done something wrong or was being mischievous. "Where are we going, Aaron?"

Laughing, he said, "Don't worry. You'll see." This was another one of Aaron's great surprises, but he wasn't sure how Ariel was going to take it. This surprise could go many different ways. It was either going to be a really great idea or a really bad one. It all depended on Ariel.

As they drove, Ariel tried to figure out where Aaron was taking her. She asked, "Can you give me a hint?"

He looked over to her and said, "All right, one hint. I didn't want to tell you anything until we got there, but I suppose I can tell you." Her eyes widened, waiting to hear what he had planned for her. "I bought us a house." Aaron waited a second for what he just said to sink in.

"How did you buy us a house? We could barely pay to go to Aruba."

He shook his head. "I know, but it was marked down, and it's a great house to start a family. It just needs a lot of work." Ariel silently sat and thought about where this house was and why it was marked down.

Finally, Aaron turned onto a very familiar street. He turned onto Elm Street. Aaron remembered the day when he'd been sleeping in a snowbank through a blizzard while Ariel was missing. As he took that turn, he recognized the red fire hydrant on which he'd hit his head. In Boston, summertime was amazing—much better than winter.

Ariel realized where they were. It was the house in which her parents had been murdered. They pulled up to the side of the lawn and got out of the car. Ariel thought about the last time she had been here. She'd had nowhere else to go.

"What do you think, honey? It won't cost much to fix it up, and it will be good as new."

Ariel thought about how her parents had died and how things would be different if they were here right now. She never would've married Aaron, and she would've grown up in the house they were looking at. Eventually, she probably would've owned this house. It really was a perfect house to start raising a family.

The only wrong thing about this house was that it was a murder house. Ariel felt uncomfortable at first to agree to live in the house. It might be haunted, or the murderer could return some night. She kept thinking about her real parents. They eventually would have wanted her to have their home.

"You bought my parents' house?"

"Yes, I called a local realtor, and luckily it was just going up for sale. She said I was the first person to call her on the house. Okay, let's go inside." He reached around Ariel holding her close to his chest as he was reassuring her that this was a good idea.

Ariel was hesitant at first, but Aaron was adamant that this was going to be the house in which they were going to live. Maybe someday they would buy a better place.

"After the investigation closed so long ago, the house was going to go up for sale anyway. I got the money from my savings account," Aaron said while they were walking up the stairs to their new house.

When they reached the front porch, Ariel was suddenly swept off her feet. She let out a laugh, knowing Aaron trying to be romantic. "Is this really necessary?"

While going up the stairs sideways and carrying Ariel, he said, "Carrying my bride into our future home? Yes, it is necessary."

Once they got to the door, they both heard cracking in the floorboards. "Um, what was that?" she asked. Confused, they held onto each other. In an instant, Aaron fell through the floorboards of the porch. They created a huge hole in their future dream home.

They both laughed uncontrollably while trying to get out of

the hole. "These boards are over twenty years old. I'll fix them up and get some new wood." The wooden boards were so rotten over the twenty years no one lived there that it couldn't hold up three hundred pounds.

"I can't believe this just happened. We're going to need more than just wood to fix this place up, by the look of it."

Aaron thought of a brilliant idea. "It's going to cost more money to hire someone to do that, than if we do it ourselves."

"What are you saying?"

Aaron smiled and said, "I'm your new carpenter." Ariel couldn't believe what he was implying. She tilted her head while still in his arms. "So you're going to fix up this whole house by yourself? I bet you don't even know how to saw wood."

He laughed, thinking that Ariel doubted him. "Hey, remember that I took woodshop when I was a junior in high school! I'm going to fix this place up with or without your help."

Ariel got up so he got pull himself out of the hole he created. She squinted at his stubbornness, wishing that he had an off button. Ariel finally agreed to go to the nearest hardware store and buy all of the stuff they needed to fix up their dream home.

Although not the greatest handyman, Aaron was determined to fix up the whole house—with or without Ariel's help.

"Aaron, I really wish you wouldn't do this. I would rather have a professional do this."

He stopped hammering new boards onto the porch and said, "What, you don't like seeing me work hard and get sweaty?" He raised his arms, and she could see the sweat marks underneath his arms. "Come here and give me a hug." Aaron started walking to her with arms open wide. The sun reflected off his face, showing he was sweating like crazy. Ariel certainly did not want to hug him.

"No! Get away from me, you sweaty beast!" She started backing up to get farther away from him.

"I'm not going anywhere until you give me a hug." He started picking up his speed to get to her. Ariel started running scared. Aaron playfully chased her around the yard. "I'm gonna get you!" he yelled to her. Eventually, he grabbed her from behind and pulled her up against his chest.

Ariel could feel his sweat through the back of her shirt. Laughing together, she said, "Are you sure you want to do this by yourself?"

Aaron looked down at her and said, "Yes, and I will upgrade our new dream home." They then shared a kiss, but a drop of sweat dripped off Aaron's forehead and onto Ariel's eyelid.

"Okay, sweaty, now get back to work." She playfully pushed him away. Then an idea entered Ariel's mind. If Aaron was confident on fixing the house all by himself, she thought she should enjoy this day. She was going to watch him do all the work by himself. He claimed he knew how to fix up the entire house, and so she was going to let him do.

She walked over the car and opened the trunk. Ariel pulled out a beach towel from her bag and laid it down on the green grass. She grabbed her sunglasses from the dashboard and lay down on the blanket.

Aaron turned around to see what she was up to. He saw that she was peacefully lying on the ground. "What are you doing?"

She lifted her sunglasses off her face and looked at him. "Oh, since you don't need my help, I thought I'd enjoy the sunshine. I don't want to lose my tan." Ariel put her arms behind her head and relaxed.

Aaron thought, Well, might as well get started with the porch.

A few hours went by, and Aaron finally fixed the porch. He put in all new floorboards that were lined up next to each other perfectly. Ariel took a short nap during that time. Eventually, she sat up and looked at his progress. She was surprised to see how he'd finished the porch without her.

Aaron then went inside. He took the keys out of his pocket and was about to unlock the door to their home. He inserted the key and turned it. As Aaron turned the doorknob to go inside, he opened the door about two feet. Then the right door of the double doors snapped off the hinges.

Aaron heard the snap and immediately caught the door, preventing it from falling on the new porch. He laid it against the side of the door frame to keep it from falling.

He put his elbow on side of the door and wiped a bead of sweat off his face. Sadly, Aaron had all his weight leaning on the door that was still on the hinges. He started to hear the same snap that he'd heard just moments ago. Within moments, the left door also snapped off the hinges.

He tried to catch it before it hit the porch, but he was too slow. It made a huge bang, and the vibration from the door hitting the porch made the other door leaning up against the frame fall on the porch as well.

Frustrated, Aaron clenched his fists. "Don't worry. I can fix that." He tried to prove Ariel wrong, still insisting that he needed no help. As a cheapskate, he also didn't want to hire anyone to do it for him.

Aaron picked up both of the doors and made them lean against the side of the house. For some reason, they wouldn't stay in place and kept sliding down.

Ariel tried to laugh quietly so he wouldn't hear her. "Do you need some help?" He didn't hear her the first time because he was too busy trying to stand the broken doors up the right way. She shouted to him again.

"Nope I got it," he said while finally getting the broken doors to stand upright. "We're going to need some new doors. Ariel, what kind of door do you think we should get?"

Still lying on her blanket, she sat upward and raised her sunglasses. "Oh, now you want my help?"

He shrugged. "No, I just wanted to know what door you wanted, honey."

She lay back down. "Oh, I know how you're not much of a home décor kind of guy. I would think you need a female opinion."

Aaron was confused as to why Ariel was playing a game with him. It was if she was toying with his mind. "Well, I could use your help with deciding on what kind of stuff to get for the house."

Ariel immediately shot up from her blanket and said, "Well, since you asked!" Then, she got in the car, expecting him to get the hint.

Aaron was still standing by the porch and wondering why she was getting in the car. He took off his tool belt and said, "Where we going?"

She looked over to him and said, "Home Depot and then Home Goods. Let's go, handyman." Aaron had a bad feeling that this trip was going to cost a lot of money. He decided to get in the car anyway.

Day by day, the house started to look brand-new. Eventually, Aaron asked for Ariel's help; he couldn't do everything by himself. After going to Home Goods, Ariel started to decorate the house a little bit, making it a little more modern. She still wanted to keep some of the original furniture though. She ripped all the white sheets off of the furniture and started to clean up the inside.

Meanwhile, Aaron tried to install the double door they had just bought. Of course, Ariel made him buy the more expensive door even though he didn't want this one. But he agreed to make her happy.

After Aaron finally installed the new double doors, he walked inside to see what Ariel was up to. He saw her in the room on the right, staring at the floor. He walked up next to her and saw what she was staring at. There was still a bloodstain from when her parents were murdered. He said, "You all right?"

She let out a sigh and said, "Do you think it's bad luck to live in a murder house? This is where my parents died. Maybe we should resell this house and move back in with Eric."

Aaron put his hands on her shoulders and looked her in the eyes.

"No way. It took me two hours to install those new doors. Don't worry. That blood stain will be gone when we get new carpeting. Eric wouldn't want us living with him again. He can finally spend some alone time with Chelsea."

Thinking about how her parents died really dampened Ariel's mood.

"Ariel, your parents would've wanted you to have this house, regardless of what happened to them. Trust me, this will be our dream home. It may not look like it yet, but I assure you it will in time."

Ariel wrapped her arms around his back as he pulled her close. Aaron knew that the house wouldn't be completely finished for about a month or two, but he decided to not tell her yet. It would probably give her one less thing to worry about.

Ariel's eyes then drifted to the old picture on the wall. They'd been hanging there for over twenty years. She walked past Aaron to get a closer look at them. They didn't come clear because they had several layers of dust on them.

Ariel removed the pictures from the wall one by one. She then put them on the stairs. "I'll put them somewhere safe for now." Aaron smiled at how she still wanted to keep those old pictures.

In that moment, the right door of the double doors slammed onto the floor. Aaron didn't want to turn around; he didn't want to see the damage. Ariel saw that there was an extra screw on the floor near the steps next to the instructions. She walked over to it and picked it up. "Do you think this screw was important?"

Aaron held several screws in his hand and realized that multiple screws were missing from the hinges. "Don't worry. I can fix this in no time." He took the other screw she was holding and continued to work on the door.

Ariel stood in the middle of the living room and thought, *Okay, where do I start?*

23

SHADE

With new floorboards and new carpeting, Ariel loved rubbing her feet on new carpet. She wore purple fuzzy socks and had a book in her hand. After admiring her new, finally finished home, she thought she should lie on the couch and read a book.

The couch was black leather and had black and white pillows on the sides. It had been a while since Ariel could relax and pick up a book. She hadn't read a good book since college.

Just as she got a few pages into her book, she saw Aaron pulling in the driveway. She folded the page and set it down on the coffee table.

As Aaron opened the door, he said, "Hey, babe." When he said that, he must have squeezed the doorknob too hard. When he entered the house, the doorknob fell off. The doorknob rolled over to Ariel's feet, and she laughed, thinking that she shouldn't let him try to build anything ever again.

"Don't worry. I can fix that." He dropped his sports bag on the stairs and picked up the doorknob. He was going to fix it immediately, but Ariel stopped him.

"Aaron, you just walked in the door. Come in and sit."

He sat on the couch next to her and said, "How was your interview with Illumination?" Illumination was an animation company that had companies all around the United States. They made movies like *Despicable Me* and *The Lorax*, and Ariel had an interview with the company just thirty minutes away from the house. The office building was in Framingham.

"I think it went well. Look, Aaron, I need to talk to you about something."

Aaron faced her and said, "Okay, shoot."

"I love our house, and I'm glad that we finally finished fixing it." She smiled.

Aaron said, "Yeah, well, except that doorknob. I'll fix that later."

She took his hands and held them in hers. She took a deep breath and said, "Well, how would you feel on redoing the room upstairs?" She smiled while looking at him raising her eyebrows.

Exhausted about thinking of doing more work on this house, Aaron said, "Yeah, we could make it my man cave."

Before he could say any more, Ariel said, "Or how about a nursery?"

Aaron was silent for a moment, and then he looked at her. "A nursery?" he asked. "We're gonna have a baby?" Ariel nodded trying not to get emotional. He hugged her before pulling away. "Oh, we're gonna be parents? We're gonna have to babyproof the whole house!" Aaron danced around the house before he returned to his wife.

Ariel laughed at how far ahead he was thinking. He bent down and started kissing her belly, sending love to his unborn child.

Time went by, and Ariel and the baby were healthy and happy—except when Ariel was hungry and when there wasn't any food in the house. She was four months along, and one could start to notice the baby bump.

She lay on the couch watching TV and eating strawberries with whipped cream. Aaron came up behind her. "I can't believe you went to the appointment without me. You still won't tell me if it's a boy or a girl!" He sat next to her on the couch while she kept eating her strawberries.

She wiped her mouth to get the whipped cream off. "Aaron, I just want you to be surprised."

He looked away, wondering why she wouldn't budge on telling him. "Can we at least start picking out baby names?"

Ariel thought, *Why not? It will have to happen eventually.* She said sure, and Aaron immediately left the room.

Knowing Aaron, she thought he would bring out his giant chalkboard from high school, which he still used to this day. He rolled it into the living room, and she saw that there was already some baby names on the board.

There was only one name to be exact. In big blue letters, it said, "Aaron Jr." Ariel was surprised only to see one name up on the board. "What if it's a girl?"

"That's what I want to know, Ariel."

Feeling pulled into a trap, she almost blurted it out. "Well, can I at least put a couple names on the board?" Aaron agreed and she walked up to the board. She erased Aaron Jr. and wrote "Boys" on one side of the board and "Girls" on the other side.

Under boys, she wrote Aaron Jr. Liam, and Jack. She stopped before going over to the girl's side and looked at him. "Now, don't make fun of my girl names." Aaron agreed, but they both knew that he would if they were awful. She wrote Talia, Shade, and Amelia. She looked at Aaron once again, hoping he wouldn't be opinionated. "Too weird?"

He shook his head, smiling. "No, I like them all. Shade is really different, but it's beautiful and very empowering. I like Shade." Ariel smiled and was grateful to have her first child.

Ariel thought Shade would be a nice name for a girl. She had a lot of memories with her godparents when they went on picnics together. It was extremely hot out in the summertime, and so they had lunch under a big tree in the park. Shade was a different name for a girl, and she was proud that she'd come up with it herself.

Five months later, Eric was driving like a mad man to get to the hospital. Eric had just received a call that Ariel had gone into labor at the hospital. Chelsea constantly yelled at him to please slow down.

When they got to the hospital, they went to the gift shop first. Not knowing the gender of the baby, Chelsea bought a teddy bear for the child.

While walking down the hallway of the hospital with Chelsea, Eric went back to the time Ariel and Aaron had gone missing in college. That was a very scary day, and Eric hadn't been in a hospital since then.

Eric and Chelsea had been together for a little while now. Even though Chelsea had known Eric and his brother for a long time, she still had a tough time telling them apart. She didn't ask which one was Aaron or Eric anymore, or at least not as often as she used to.

As they turned the corner into Ariel's room, Eric got a gust of excitement at walking into that room. He saw Aaron facing away from him, holding his child. Aaron turned around with the biggest smile on his face.

Eric looked down at the child and saw there was a pink hat on its head. "Eric, meet your niece. Shade, meet your Uncle Eric." He then gave Shade to Eric to hold.

Ariel rested in bed after many hours of labor. She watched how Aaron gently placed her daughter into Eric's arms for the first time.

"She's so beautiful," Eric said as he watched the toddler yawn while her eyes were still closed. He had never seen anything so small and delicate. "Well, hello there."

Chelsea said as she stood behind Eric and looked at Shade. "Welcome to the world little one."

Eric looked away and saw how happy Chelsea was looking at his new niece. He thought that someday he wanted to have kids of his own. "Shade? That's different."

Aaron looked over to Ariel and said, "Yes, but it's a good different, and it suits her beauty perfectly."

Ariel looked at Aaron again and said, "We're going to be amazing parents. Promise me one thing, though." Aaron leaned down next to her to hear what she had to say. "Promise me that we're gonna stay with one for a while."

Aaron understood what she was implying. She wanted to spend time with Shade for a while until they added onto their family. "Yeah, sure," he agreed. Little did they know that was only their first, and they were going to welcome many more into the world.

24

ADDING ON

Elm Street was the street where Ariel and Aaron had made lots of memories, from the day when Ariel had seen her parents' house for the first time to now, where Aaron had completely upgraded the entire house.

Before Ariel and Aaron moved in, the house on Elm Street was small and incredibly damaged. Now, it was modern and a humble, happy home for Ariel and Aaron, along with their four children.

Putting an addition on the house was not easy at first. Aaron stood by his stubbornness and wanted to build the entire addition by himself. It took him five years to finish, but he finally finished their dream house.

When they bought the house, it was in the middle of the yard. Now, the addition reached almost the end of the street on the right side.

It was a Friday morning in the Smith residence. Shade was all grown up now and was just finishing putting on her makeup. "You're growing up too fast," her father always told her. It was the last day of school, and she was going to be a junior in the fall.

Shade felt like today was going to be the day her crush finally asked her out. She wanted to look nice for the day. She sat at her desk and put on her makeup. On her purple painted walls, there was a mirror, and she looked at herself while applying mascara.

With big green eyes and long brown hair, Shade felt confident about starting her junior year in the fall. Everyone said that junior year was the hardest, but Shade was eager to get to it.

She wished she could play hooky and go to the skateboard park with her friends. Her dad would have her head if he found out she'd skipped the last day of school. She's just turned sixteen, and she hoped that Jonny, her crush, would ask her out on a date. She also hoped that her dad would let her go out with him. Her dad had never let her out on a date before, but she hadn't asked him in a while. *Maybe he will this time,* she thought.

Her mom always said, "You can go out on a date, but you have to go ask your dad first." Now, she believed that she was old enough to enter a new chapter of her life.

Banging on the door was her little brother Liam. She yelled, "Don't break my door, Liam!" He didn't stop banging until she opened it. Shade got out from her chair and decided to let him in. She would soon regret that.

She opened the door and saw Liam standing in front of her with a smile on his face. She could tell that she had something to say. "What?"

"Whoa, that's a lot of makeup. If you're still trying to impress Jonny, it's not going to work." Liam was in eighth grade but had the arrogance of a freshman, which was what grade he'd be next year.

"Don't you have someone else you can annoy?"

Liam said, "Yes, but it's not as fun when I do it to someone else." Shade let out a growl and tried to close the door, but Liam was stronger than her. "Look I'm just trying to help you out, Shade. Next year, with me being the school's first starting freshman, I can talk to Jonny for you." He smoothed back his greasy blonde hair, trying to act cool. Liam was the star of his middle school basketball team. Shade was secretly jealous of his basketball abilities.

If Liam tried to do a trick on her skateboard, he wouldn't succeed after numerous tries. "Having a good heart is more important than being an athletic star," her mom always told her. Shade related to her mom because she wasn't the most coordinated person either.

Shade looked at all her skateboarding trophies on her shelf above her bed. She was grateful that she did have some athletic ability in her. While Liam was talking, she kept daydreaming about Jonny. Maybe they would ride there skateboards off into the sunset …

Shade quickly snapped back to reality upon hearing her mother's voice. "Kids, breakfast." Liam quickly ran out of her sister's room. Shade grabbed her backpack off the back of her door and closed the door behind her.

She was almost run over by her other little brother, Jack, who quickly ran down the hallway. "Coming, Mom!" he said. She soon heard tumbling down the stairs. "You okay, Jack?" She walked toward the top of the stairs and looked down.

Jack was steadying himself and trying not to fall again. "Yeah, I'm fine." Then he continued down the stairs to eat breakfast. Jack was eleven and had a very high pain tolerance. One time when they were at the lake, he got stung by a bee, and he didn't even notice. Shade noticed it because there was a huge bulge on his back.

Shade's favorite sibling of all was her little sister, Amelia. Mainly it was because she was the quietest and the most cooperative. Amelia was beyond adorable and very smart for her age. Her mind was full of curiosity for a six-year-old. Amelia came behind her big sister and poked her in the back. Shade turned around to see her kind smile and bright eyes.

Amelia said, "Can you braid my hair?" Shade agreed to after breakfast, and they walked down the stairs together.

While going down the stairs, Shade realized how old Amelia had gotten. She felt like it was yesterday that her mom had brought

Amelia home from the hospital. Shade held her hand so she didn't trip down the stairs like Jack.

Once they entered the kitchen, Shade picked up Amelia and put on the bar stool. Then she sat in between her two brothers. Shade watched her mother cook. Ariel made a huge batch of scrambled eggs and bacon. She gave everybody the same amount of bacon and scrambled eggs on each plate.

"Morning, Mom," Shade said.

Ariel turned around and said, "Morning."

Ariel had aged over the years, but she still had the same smile and charm. She had strands gray hair just starting to come in, and she had her hair up in a tight bun. With a black sweater and dress pants, Ariel was getting ready to go to work.

When Ariel served her kids breakfast, Shade realized that Ariel was still wearing her white bracelet. Shade had never seen a day when her mother didn't have it on.

Shade took time eating her breakfast while her siblings gobbled up every bite. Curious about her mom's bracelet, she decided to ask her about it. Once her siblings left the kitchen area she said, "Mom, you never told me about that."

Ariel turned around from washing the dishes. "About what, honey?" Shade pointed to the bracelet she been wearing for so many years. "Oh, this. This bracelet was a gift from your father." She put the dishes down and laid her wrist on the counter for Shade to see. "Your father made this for me when we were in high school."

Shade's eyes widened. *She's had that bracelet all this time?*

Ariel continued. "Your father is the most stubborn man I've ever met." Shade smiled knowing that was true. "He knew that we would get married someday, and he made this for me to give to me on our wedding day."

Shade was touched by their love for each other. It was the kind of love that didn't come around very often. Shade asked, "You've never taken it off?"

Ariel shook her head and said, "I don't think I've ever taken it off, other then when I get in the shower."

Shade looked more closely at the bracelet and saw the sliver letters engraved on it. She saw the *AA* on it in silver writing and said, "That's so sweet. That's a symbol of love."

Aaron came around the corner. He had glasses now and deeper lines on his forehead. In a suit and tie and hard shoes, he entered the kitchen. "What's a symbol of love?" he asked while giving Ariel a kiss on the cheek.

"Oh, just when you made me this." Ariel raised her hand, showing that she still wore it.

"Oh, yeah. It feels like yesterday that I gave that to you, doesn't it?"

"Yeah, it does," Ariel replied.

Aaron grabbed a cup of coffee and went into the other room to play with his other kids before they went to school. It was something that he did almost every morning.

"Speaking of love, has that cute boy Jonny asked you out yet?" Ariel asked.

Shade was surprised that her mom was bringing up this subject again. "Mom, he probably won't ever ask me out." She grabbed her dishes and put them in the sink.

As she did so, her mom said, "What? A girl like you? Come on, Shade."

Shade turned around. "No, *you* come on, Mom. He has never looked at me twice."

Before she could check out of this conversation, Ariel grabbed her by the shoulders. "Now, you listen to me. You have so many good qualities that you don't realize. You're five ten, you're pretty, and you're pretty awesome on a skateboard. The trophies in your room say so."

Blushing at her moms words, Shade said, "Only four state championships."

"Come on, Shade. Those are huge accomplishments! I could never do what you do on a skateboard when I was your age."

Realizing that she was pretty awesome, she said, "Thanks, Mom." They hugged.

Amelia came into the kitchen. "Shade, can you braid my hair now?"

"I suppose," Shade said to her sister. She sat on the couch while Amelia sat in between her legs. Shade parted her sister's blonde hair into three sections before she started the braid.

Ariel peeked around the corner, watching her two daughters interact with each other. She thought back to when Aaron would braid her hair for fun when they were six. He wasn't good on the first couple of tries, but he eventually got the hang of it.

Ariel thought about how close her daughters were, and she smiled. Then she thought about how Liam and Jack always got into fights almost every day. It'd be over something so small, like when Jack ate the last ice cream sandwich, and Liam was furious about it.

"All right, can I have everyone in the living room, please?" Ariel entered the middle of the room, waiting for the boys to come in and listen. Aaron, Liam, and Jack came in the living room, waiting to hear what she had to say.

"It is the end of another school year." Everyone cheered with happiness and relief that another school year was past them. "We will be having our yearly end of the school year barbeque."

Instantly, Amelia stood up with her new braided hair and said, "Are Uncle Eric and Aunt Chelsea coming?"

"Yes, they'll come around after school."

Eric and Chelsea got busy after they got married. They had a two twin girls, Riley and Delaney, who were Amelia's age. They weren't identical, and so everyone could tell them apart. Then they had two older boys. One was Jack's age, and his name was Connor. Their oldest boy was fifteen, and his name was Evan. All of Eric's children received his hair genes, with the same texture and shade of brown.

Amelia was overjoyed when she heard that her cousins were coming over. She started jumping up a down uncontrollably. Ariel laughed at how happy see was, and then she looked out the window and saw that the school bus was here. "Okay, everybody. Last day of school. Let's go!"

Shade, Liam, and Jack went to the same school. The bottom floor was for grades six through eight, and the top floor was for high school students. The first bus pulled up to the end of Elm Street.

Jack and Liam had a race to who could get to the bus first. It was the same door that Aaron had tried to fix for years. Luckily, he finally did.

Shade walked to the bus while putting her ear buds in to listen to music. She watched how her brothers almost tripped over each other to see who could get to the bus first.

While getting into his car, Aaron laughed as the bus drove away. He'd gotten a job as the school's high school basketball coach. He loved spending his day with all the kids on the team, and he got a chance to see his own kids during the day.

He blew a kiss to his wife and daughter while pulling out of the driveway. Ariel and Amelia waved goodbye while standing on the porch. Amelia started jumping up and down on the porch.

Aaron went back to a memory sixteen years ago, when Aaron had carried Ariel into the house and the floorboards had given out from under them.

Ariel couldn't believe how energetic Amelia was. For a little girl, she had a big heart full of love and happiness.

"Mommy, do you have to work today?"

She looked down at her daughter and said, "Oh, yes. Today is a big workday for Mommy."

Amelia started jumping up and down while holding her mom's hands. "Why is today such a big work day?"

She chuckled at her daughter's questions. Her curiosity amazed Ariel because she hadn't been as curious when she'd been that age. "Because today Mommy might get a big promotion at work."

Stumbling over the new word, Amelia said, "What's a promotion?"

Ariel laughed at her trying to pronounce big words. "A promotion is where I get moved higher up in a position at work."

Amelia stopped jumping and thought about what her mother had just said. Her answer to that was, "My mommy must be really smart."

Ariel smiled. Even though she was not Einstein, Amelia boosted her confidence. She remembered when she'd been little and Eric had done all her homework for her. He could've said no, but he couldn't turn down free homework.

Half an hour went by, and Amelia's school bus pulled up to the end of Elm Street. Amelia played on the steps and didn't realize her bus was here. Ariel said, "Okay, Amelia, last day of school. The bus is here." Amelia stopped playing on the steps and turned around to see the big bus waiting for her.

Ariel grabbed the backpack from inside the house and gave it to her daughter. Then she watched Amelia walk to the bus from the house. Before Amelia got on the bus, she turned around to wave at her mom. RIEL waved back to her. Once the bus drove away, Ariel had to get ready for possibly the most important work day of her life.

Ariel skimmed the beads of her bracelet on her wrist with her opposite hand. She'd admired it for so many years. It was a symbol of her and Aaron's love. She couldn't believe how fast time flew by. She felt like it was only yesterday Aaron had given this to her.

25

TOGETHER

While going to work, Ariel felt a huge amount of pressure. Today was going to be the day her boss was going to choose someone to be head director of the company. That meant before everything was transferred over to Pixar or Disney, the head director would have to make sure everything was in tip-top shape.

Of everyone in the company, Ariel thought no one else should get the position except her. She'd been with the company for fifteen years, and no one was more qualified than her to do the job right.

In Ariel's mind, she had to step up her game with the new interns coming into the company for the summer. She thought that if she got the job, it would be great for her and her family. Playing an important role in the company meant a higher salary as well, which would be great for her and the kids.

Shade was just settling into her seat in her final math class of the year. She sat down in the back left corner, waiting for Jonny to enter the room. Someday she'd get revenge on the three golden girls in her class. Some said they were the girls who got all the nice-looking guys.

The three girls were laughing about something, and Shade wondered what. They were the three most fake girls she had ever seen. They all dyed their hair golden blonde. She could tell because she could see the roots coming in at the tops of their heads, and their eyebrows were brown from their real hair color.

To go along with the fakeness, they had fake sparkly nails. *How can one grab anything or even write with those things?* Shade thought. She definitely couldn't do skateboard tricks with those things on. They all looked like female Edward Scissorhands.

Jonny entered the classroom. The golden girls took notice, and one decided to approach him. Victoria was the head of the golden girls and bossed the other two girls around like they were her servants. Yet she still claimed they were her friends.

As Victoria and Jonny were talking, Shade's best friend, Mara, sat down at her desk next to her. "Hey, Shade, what's going on?"

Shade put her head down on her desk and said, "Victoria is making her move on Jonny. That's what's going on." She covered her face, trying to not look. Victoria's personality was not for Shade's taste. She couldn't stand Victoria's fake smile and dead shark eyes— especially when she was trying to move in on her crush.

Mara tried reading lips to figure out the conversation. Jonny put his hand up as he tried to get away from Victoria. Jonny shut her down and walked back to his desk.

Mara poked Shade in the shoulder and said, "Jonny just shut down Victoria!"

Shade shot up from her desk to see a sad look on Victoria's face. *To see that Jonny rejected her means that he probably knows what type of person she really is. She may look pretty on the outside, but inside her soul is dead and ugly.*

"Has Jonny spoken to you yet?" Mara asked.

Shade still couldn't believe that he'd moved away from Victoria. "No, he hasn't, and it's the end of another school year."

Mara could feel her friend's pain when Shade so badly wanted something to happen. "Don't worry. He might ask you out after class."

Shade answered, "I hope so."

Meanwhile, downstairs in that same building, Jack and Liam were getting ready for PE. It was the last day of school, and so they knew their PE was going to be extra fun. Liam hoped the teacher would take it easy on him today and not make him do pull-ups for not listening or for goofing off with his friends.

Liam didn't care too much for his PE teacher. Today, though, he was like a different person. Instead of putting everyone through grilling exercises and extreme workouts, the teacher simply let the kids have fun today.

They had fun games for today's PE class. The teacher divided everyone up in teams for relay races and team trust exercises. Every time a team won, he would give that team one point. Whoever had the most points at the end of the period would win a secret surprise.

Mr. Durell had a secret surprise planned for the team that won. He was going to give every kid on the winning team free Celtics merchandise. He'd ordered a bunch of T-shirts in every size, as well as some socks, mugs, and other cool Celtics merchandise. He felt bad for the losing teams, and so he decided to give all the Celtics merchandise to every single kid who came to PE today. After that day, he wasn't known as the grilling PE teacher anymore. That made his day, seeing all the kids happy and grateful to have him as their teacher. It was a teacher's dream to see all their students happy.

Liam was extremely shocked about this surprise. He had no idea that Mr. Durell had planned this for their last day of school.

Mr. Durell was the buzz of the school for the day. Aaron heard about how everyone got Celtic's merchandise for coming to PE today, and he wished he'd gone to visit him. *Wait a minute—that's gotta be a different teacher. Did Mr. Durell get fired?* Aaron laughed, thinking that maybe the kids had fun today in P.E.

Aaron had always thought he had to give back to others. When he was fourteen, his history teacher told the class about how kids lived in Africa, not having food or decent houses. It broke Aaron's heart. Ever since then, his outlook on life had changed completely.

It warmed Aaron's heart when he heard that Mr. Durell had given something to all the kids. He'd thought that Mr. Durell wasn't a very chummy person to begin with, but Aaron had been wrong all this time.

The school day finished. Kids exploded from the school doors, rushing out into the front of the school.

Shade walked by herself, making her way to her bus to go home. Mara waved goodbye to her as she got on her own bus. Shade continued walking to her bus until she heard a voice calling her name. "Shade! Shade, wait up!" She turned around to see Jonny a few feet behind her, catching up to her. She was almost speechless that Jonny had said her name.

Jonny said, "Shade, do you wanna hang out with me and couple friends tonight?"

Shade swallowed and said, "You and some friends?"

Jonny smiled. "Yeah. I want you to come with me to the skating rink. You're the only girl I know who is sick on a skateboard. It'll be fun."

She smiled at the compliment. "I'd love to, but I have to ask my parents first." She was concerned about what her dad would say about going out with Jonny to hang out with a bunch of guys at the skating rink.

"Okay, text me, and I'll come and pick you up."

"Sounds good."

He looked into her eyes once again before leaving to get on his bus. Shade almost couldn't believe it. Was she dreaming? She was very content with her day and how it had turned out.

She turned around and almost tripped while getting on the bus, still thinking about their conversation. She went to the back of the bus and sat in her usual spot. She slumped down in her seat, let out a sigh of relief, and smiled.

She looked up at the ceiling of the bus and couldn't stop smiling. Chuckling, she couldn't believe what had just happened. She fantasized about that very moment so many times, and today it finally happened.

She looked out the window and saw everyone from the school getting on their bus. This year was finally over, and it couldn't have ended any better.

Liam saw his sister smiling uncontrollably from a few rows away. She had never had a bigger smile on her face then she did right now. It appeared that she felt like she was in her own little world. "Hey, sis, did Jonny just ask you out?"

Shade smiled and nodded, hoping he wouldn't blab to everyone on the bus.

He said, "Does Dad know?" Shade shook her head, worried what her dad might think. Her smile faded at her brother's next words.

"Good luck. You're gonna need it!."

Shade replayed her conversation with Jonny over and over in her head. She texted Mara and told her what had happened. She was sweating, and her heart pounded fast while she thought about what on earth she was going to do to convince her dad to let her go out with Jonny.

During the ride home on the bus, Shade stared out her window with a smile on her face, thinking about what she would wear tonight. She thought, *I'm just going to the roller rink. I can wear jeans and a shirt with my black and my red flannel.* She was relieved that she wouldn't have to dress up and be fancy, because she was more comfortable in regular clothes. Being fancy was not her thing.

Before she knew it, the bus was pulling up to Elm Street. Shade grabbed her stuff and got off the bus. As she walked down the steps of the bus, she realized that her dad's car was in the driveway. When she entered the house, she saw Uncle Eric and Aunt Chelsea on the couch. It was a big deal to the Smith family at the end of every school year to have a big family cookout. Hugs were given, and there was plenty of laughter with everybody together.

Amelia came home from school and immediately rushed over to her cousins Rylie and Delancy. She hadn't seen them since Easter. Shade was overwhelmed by a lot of people in the living room: her sister and brothers, her four cousins, Aunt Chelsea and Uncle Eric, and her mom and dad.

She walked over to Aaron and whispered," Dad, can I talk to you for a second?"

He said, "Sure." They walked into the dining room. Aaron was worried that something might be wrong because Shade never asked to talk to him in private before.

As she walked behind her dad, she couldn't help but feel sad. She had a feeling that he would say no to her going out with Jonny. She felt as if he had already said no to her, and she hadn't even asked him yet. She could feel it in her gut.

Aaron sat down in one of the chairs closest to her and looked at his daughter. Shade fidgeted with her hands, trying to get the words out of her mouth. She closed her eyes and said a small prayer inside her head.

"Okay, Dad. I have to ask you something."

"Okay," Aaron said, wondering what she had to ask him that was so important. He kept an open mind and listened to what she had to say.

"Jonny Stevenson asked my out on a date today." Her heart beat in her throat while she waited to hear his response. Her mom would've been fine with her going out on a date when she was fourteen. Her dad had put a stop to it, though.

He raised an eyebrow, thinking about what she'd just said. "Oh, really?"

Shade was surprised that he didn't say no immediately. "Yes. He wants to come pick me and go to the skating rink tonight. I know it's our family cookout, but I was hoping he could pick me up afterward?"

Aaron looked at his daughter, still remembering when he'd taught her how to ride a bike for the first time. He remembered the first time she'd done a trick on a skateboard. She wasn't that little girl anymore—she had grown up. It was almost like time flashed before his eyes. *Soon enough, even little Amelia will be all grown up.*

Before Shade could say anything else, he said, "Yeah, sure. You can go out with Jonny. After you visit with your family, though."

Who are you, and what have you done with my dad? Shade thought. Tonight was the night she had been thinking about for years. Now, it was finally going to happen. Smiling, she rushed to hug her dad while he still sat in the chair. "Thank you!"

He returned the hug, happy to see that she was exited. They rejoined the rest of the family.

The cookout started, and everyone ventured outside to enjoy the sunset through the trees. Aaron manned the grill, mainly because he wouldn't let anyone else touch his precious grill. He cooked burgers, steak, and sausages. Eric and Chelsea had brought dessert, a delicious homemade cheesecake. This time Eric didn't buy it; Chelsea made from scratch. Eric thought it would be a good idea. Chelsea knew that Eric wasn't much of a chef; he could cook or prepare only a handful of dishes—if he didn't burn them while he tried to cook them.

The last time he'd seen that kind of dessert was when Aaron had put a diamond ring in the cheesecake the night he'd proposed to Ariel. Upon seeing another cheesecake, Aaron went back to that memory, and it was the happiest day of his life.

Amelia and he cousins ran around the front yard, trying to run away from Jack, and Liam. The boys were chasing them around just because. Meanwhile, Shade talked to Connor and Evan on the porch. She blabbed to them about her skateboarding trophies that she had won while also trying to be humble about them.

They were in awe of her talent because neither of them could skateboard. They were impressed by what she could do on a skateboard. Shade thought tricks were no big deal, but it was a big deal to people who couldn't do anything on a skateboard.

Ariel caught up with Chelsea and Eric. They sat down at a table on the front porch, laughed and remembered old memories like they were yesterday, and enjoyed delicious iced tea.

The sun was almost down, and they could still see the roaring colors in the sky. Orange and red soon disappeared from the sky; the sun had gone down for the day, to return in the morning.

Shade looked over to her mother and saw how close her family was. They sure had known each other for a long time. Her dad kept getting caught up in their conversations, and he almost ended up burning the burgers.

Shade then pulled out her phone from her pocket to text Jonny, but she got a text from him first. *It's weird how sometimes you think about a person and want to contact them, and they end up contacting you first.* Shade was startled by it.

The text said, "Hey, Shade. What time do you want me to pick you up?"

She smiled as she was replied. "I'll be ready around nine." She hit the send button and put her phone back in her pocket.

She watched as the sun continued going down behind the trees. She had to wait another two hours before Jonny came to pick her up. The waiting part was painful, but she knew it would be worth the wait.

When you first meet a person, you try not to judge them. The way he looks, how he talks, or how he walks. None of that matters. What matters is what's inside. She smiled, *That's why Jonny turned down Victoria. He truly knew what kind of person she is. She is a monster, and he wants nothing to do with her.*

Jonny saw her as a decent human being and a cool girl. Shade had spent years contemplating whom she would want to aspire to be.

She made the right choice because she decided to be herself, and that was a gem. *Being anyone but yourself is just wasting time on this earth.*

The burgers were almost done, and Aaron remembered something that Ariel had run by him this morning: there was a new position at her work. She had been nervous about getting the promotion. He wondered why she hadn't brought it up since she'd come home.

He closed the grill, thinking the burgers had a few more minutes to cook. "Hey, Ariel, did you get that promotion today?"

Ariel ended her conversation with Chelsea and walked over to him. She had a concerned look on her face that implied something went wrong. She grabbed his hand and looked into his eyes. She remembered how he used to play stupid tricks and mean pranks on her when they were younger.

"Yeah?" Aaron could tell by the look on her face that she didn't get the promotion.

"Yeah, I got the promotion!"

His frown instantly turned into a laughing smile. "You tried to trick me, didn't you?" Aaron was surprised at how Ariel had faked him out. *I guess I deserve it for all the pranks I did to Ariel so many years ago.*

He hugged her and laughed when he realized that she'd gotten him. "You've been working on your acting skills, haven't you?"

She nodded.

He thought something a lot worse might have happened at work today, like she had lost her job or something. The way she'd looked at him had made him think the worst, but that was just her acting skills.

Aaron shook his head. Ariel always kept him on his toes; she'd learned how to do that over the years. Mainly it was by messing with him, even with the most important things.

Aaron was happy that she'd gotten the promotion and gave her a kiss. Then he turned back to man the grill. He was still smiling, and

Ariel knew what he was thinking. He was probably thinking of the worst situation. She sat back down in her chair and started talking to Chelsea again. They returned to their conversation about how Ariel couldn't believe Shade was going be a junior in high school.

Shade witnessed how much her parents loved each other. They laughed and played together, and she could see their love when talking with one another. It was true love, and that was something Shade hoped to find one day.

As Ariel sat down, she remembered she hadn't gotten the mail yet today. She got up from her chair and proceeded down the stairs.

Ariel was almost run over by Jack trying to get away from his older brother. They were playing some made-up game like they usually did. She remembered when she would make up fun games to play when she was their age.

She reached inside the mailbox and grabbed the mail. She scanned through the mail to see if there was anything important. There wasn't, but then she looked up.

Ariel saw her two sons, Liam and Jack, running around playfully. Amelia was playing with her dolls on the ground with Rylie and Delancy. Shade was talking to Evan and Connor on the porch, laughing about something Evan said and playfully elbowing him.

She couldn't believe that her baby girl was going on her very first date this evening. Ariel recalled the happy dance they'd shared in the kitchen when Shade had told her Jonny had asked her out.

Ariel was surprised Aaron had given her permission. He was so overprotective of all his kids, but he and Shade had a very special connection. Shade was his firstborn child. The happiest day in his life was when Shade had been born, but he'd never admit it.

To the left, she saw the man she loved getting the burgers off the grill. She saw Eric and Chelsea so happy together. She remembered how Chelsea had stood up for her in school, and how she had been her only friend at the time.

Ariel had flashbacks to when her godparents took care of her, and how they'd died. Then she gazed upon the house in which she was living. Aaron had fixed up the place all by his arrogant self. Putting on an addition made the house even more beautiful.

Every day, she could feel her real parents looking down at her, guiding her through life's obstacles. She felt good about living in their house. It gave Ariel closure, and she still kept those old pictures from the day her and Aaron had moved in. She still had them in her closet to this very day.

Her parents' killer was never found. It was filed as an unsolved case, but Ariel had an unsolved case of her own. A case called life.

Just behind the house, lurking in the woods, was a dark figure. He was dressed in all black, even preventing his face from being seen by wearing a ski mask. He could hear laughter coming from the front of the house. He wanted to get in a closer position, but he would be at risk of being seen. As he was about to move, Ariel came around the back of the house to get something. The suspicious character stayed still and watched her from a distance.

She walked to the middle of the backyard and bent down to pick up Amelia's toys from earlier. Ariel stuck the mail underneath her arm that she had just received and picked up her toys.

She grabbed a plastic horse, along with two cowgirls that Amelia had played with not long ago. As she bent up, her eyes fixated on the dark figure standing in the woods.

The man dressed in dark clenched his fists, hoping that he wouldn't get caught. After all these years, Ariel had finally found the person who'd killed her parents. He'd been watching over her very closely since she'd been in college.

Ariel was unsure if what she was looking at was a part of a tree, or if it was just a dark shadow. She squinted, trying to get a better look. It appeared to look like a man hiding behind the tree. As she was about to get a closer look, she heard, "Hey, Ariel, whatcha doing?"

Aaron stood next to her and saw what she was looking at. She dropped all of the toys that were in her arms, including the mail.

"I was just trying to clean up the yard, and I thought I saw someone."

Aaron bent down and helped Ariel pick up all the mail that was on the ground. "Someone where?"

She stood upright. "Right over there." But as she looked at that same tree, the dark figure had disappeared. It was as if the figure had vanished in seconds. She was confused as to why a shadow of a man had been standing behind a tree and then suddenly was gone in a flash.

"I swear I just saw someone." She frowned, wondering if she was starting to see things that were not real.

"Hun, it was probably nothing, just a shadow."

Ariel was sure that she'd seen someone out in the woods, but whoever it was disappeared. *And who would want to lurk behind my house?* she thought.

She and Aaron turned around and walked back to the front of the house to rejoin their family. The sun had just gone down, and it got dark quick.

What Ariel didn't know was that man was still in the woods behind her house. Curious to know if he was spotted, he thought that tonight would be the perfect night. After all these years, he had never been caught for the crime he'd committed over forty years ago. All he had to do was sit and wait for the right moment.

When everyone decided to bring the party inside the house, Ariel stayed outside on the porch by herself. She looked beyond the pillars of her porch and into the woods. She saw darkness surround the yard, and she heard branches cracking as the wind blew them around. The full moon shined brightly down on the world.

She could no longer see far out in front of her. The only brightness was the light from the porch. Meanwhile, she could see and hear cars driving by Elm Street. The cars' headlights would shine on

Elm Street for no more than a moment as they drove by. Then the darkness returned. Ariel heard an owl hoot in the distance, and she realized that she was completely alone.

"Mom, what are you doing out here all by yourself?"

Ariel turned around to see her daughter Amelia peeking her head around the double doors. "Oh, honey, I just needed alone time. I'll come in a bit."

Amelia backed up from the door and then shut it. Ariel turned back to looking out into the darkness. Her gut told her that someone was out there. She simply just tell herself that the shadow she'd seen earlier was nothing, because it was something.

Ever since Shade had been born, Ariel had made a promise to herself that she would always be around for her children. She never wanted her kids to feel the pain of losing their parents at such a young age. Ariel had experienced that pain firsthand.

She exercised by weaving it into her busy schedule. It was hard at times, but she was lucky that she had a gym a few miles from her work. *You don't always love going to the gym, but you love how you feel after you come out.*

She took one more last look and then went back inside. Little did she know that the man in black was watching her stand on the porch. Hidden behind a bush, he managed to get a better look of the house from a distance. He blended in perfectly with the bush so that no one could spot him. He remained behind that bush until he felt that the moment had arrived.

Unsettled, Ariel remembered that Shade was going out tonight with Jonny. With a peculiar individual possibly nearby, she almost didn't want anyone leaving the house at all.

She saw Shade coming downstairs and smelled perfume. Shade stuck her phone in her back pocket while she grabbed her wallet off of the table.

Ariel questioned herself as to whether she should not let Shade go out tonight. *Unless it's just my own paranoia, and there is really no one in the woods after all,* she thought. Ariel saw Jonny pull up in front of the house and honk the horn.

"Okay, I'll be back before eleven," Shad said.

Ariel didn't know why, but before Shade went out the door, she grabbed Shade by her arm just as she was about to leave. "Shade please be back by curfew. Call me if you get into any trouble."

Shade rolled her eyes, thinking her mom was overreacting. "Mom, don't worry. We're just going to the skate park." She smiled back at her mom, so excited and eager to leave. She kept thinking, *Come on, Mom. Don't become protective over me now. I'm only going to the skate park. What could possibly go wrong?*

Shade turned away from her mom to say goodnight to Amelia, but she was already sound asleep on the couch. She'd had a very eventful day and was exhausted from playing with her cousins. They too were starting to nod off while lying next to Eric.

Shade grabbed her skateboard out from behind the couch. "Bye! I'll see you later."

Ariel let her daughter walk out the door. She watched from the window as Shade put her skateboard in the back seat of the car and then got in the front seat. Jonny drove away slowly, stopped at the end of Elm Street, and then turned right, driving toward the skate park. Ariel had a bad feeling about letting her daughter walk out that door.

Aaron got up from the couch, seeing that Ariel was worried about Shade going out by herself. Everyone else was just sitting on the long couch and watching TV. "Sweetheart, she'll be fine. I'll wait up for her tonight." He kissed her on the cheek.

Her arms were still crossed, and she anxiously watched her daughter in the passenger seat of the car that drove away from the house. "Oh, I'm gonna stay up too. There's no way I'm falling asleep for a while, anyway."

Eric said, "Well, I think it's time for us to head out. Thank you so much for having this get together. We need to do it more often."

Chelsea came in and hugged Ariel and Aaron. Eric, still on the couch, had to wake his daughter to get up and go in the car.

"Oh, absolutely. It was fun for the kids." Ariel hugged Eric goodbye as he got off the couch.

"Rylie, Delancy, let's go home. Come on, boys."

Rubbing their eyes, Rylie and Delancy got up off the couch. Connor and Evan soon followed their parents out the door after saying goodbye to their aunt and uncle.

Ariel shut the door behind them and turned to see Aaron carrying Amelia upstairs to put her to bed. Amelia rested her head on his shoulders while her legs wrapped around his waist. Aaron walked up the stairs carrying his angel in his arms, and Ariel sat back on the couch with Liam and Jack.

She was tired, but not tired enough to go to sleep. She wanted to stay up until she knew that Shade had made it home safe.

A few minutes later, Aaron reappeared from upstairs and sat down next to her. "She's out like a light." He grabbed the blanket that was on top of the couch and threw it over himself and Ariel. She snuggled up next to his chest while they watched a movie.

Halfway through the movie, she said, "Do you think someone was out in the woods watching us today? I just had a funny feeling."

"No, don't worry, honey. It was just shadow. I'd like to see someone try to spy on us. They won't get very far. I'll protect this family for as long as I live."

As they were about to kiss, Liam said, "Ew! You guys aren't going to kiss right now, are you?"

Ariel turned away from Aaron and said, "Well, if you don't want to watch, I suggest you leave the room." She raised her eyebrows and smiled, knowing what their answer was going to be.

She turned back to Aaron and heard both of them say, "Okay, goodnight." They dashed out of the living room and upstairs to go to bed.

Aaron laughed at Ariel's plan to get them to go to bed. They heard footsteps patter up the stairs at a rapid pace, and soon their bedroom doors slammed shut.

Ariel laid her head back on his chest and continued watching the movie. Aaron planted a delicate kiss on the top of her head and rubbed her back, knowing that summer had finally begun. Being in Boston during the summer was paradise.

Then again, paradise is wherever you're happy right? When the snow finally melts, the city gleams as lights fill the city. And during the day, you can walk or run the Charles River for hours on end.

Aaron was excited that the kids were going to be around the house a lot more. Ariel, on the other hand, was still worried about the odd shadow she'd seen in the back yard. She swore she saw somebody hiding behind a tree. Her gut told her that someone was lurking around, but Aaron reassured her that she'd seen nothing. Whoever it was it had been gone in an instant. *It's just my eyes seeing things,* she thought.

The mysterious man made his way to the skate park, which was only a few miles from Elm Street. As he walked down the street, not many people would think that he was a person who was a demented criminal. He didn't carry himself to look or act like someone who was not wired right in the brain.

He was a vicious mastermind who had been roaming the streets for decades, keeping a close eye on Ariel her entire life. He was a slick and careful criminal who was able to cover his tracks so well that he was never caught. Now, he was ready to strike again.

About the Author

Syd Sullivan began writing at age fourteen. She lives in a small town in New Hampshire. Writing is her passion along with her love of basketball. This is her debut book.

CPSIA information can be obtained
at www.ICGtesting.com
Printed in the USA
BVHW031912050220
571543BV00001B/54

9 781480 871168